THE AUTHOR

ETHEL WILSON was born in Port Elizabeth, South Africa, in 1888. She was taken to England at the age of two after her mother died. Seven years later her father died, and in 1898 she came to Vancouver to live with her maternal grandmother. She received her teacher's certificate from the Vancouver Normal School in 1907 and taught in many local elementary schools until her marriage in 1921.

In the 1930s Wilson published a few short stories and began a series of family reminiscences which were later transformed into *The Innocent Traveller*. Her first published novel, *Hetty Dorval*, appeared in 1947, and her fiction career ended fourteen years later with the publication of her story collection, *Mrs. Golightly and Other Stories*. Through her compassionate and often ironic narration, Wilson explores in her fiction the moral lives of her characters.

For her contribution to Canadian literature, Wilson was awarded the Canada Council Medal in 1961 and the Lorne Pierce Medal of the Royal Society of Canada in 1964. Her husband died in 1966, and she spent her later years in seclusion and ill-health.

Ethel Wilson died in Vancouver in 1980.

HETTY DORVAL

ETHEL WILSON

AFTERWORD BY
NORTHROP FRYE

Library and Archives Canada Cataloguing in Publication

Wilson, Ethel, 1888-1980
        Hetty Dorval / Ethel Wilson ; with an afterword by Northrop Frye.

(New Canadian library)
Originally publ.: Toronto : Macmillan of Canada, 1947.
ISBN 978-0-7710-8889-6

        I. Title.   I. Series.

PS8545.I62H4 2008   C813'.52   C2008-900797-2

We acknowledge the financial support of the Government of Canada through the Book Publishing Industry Development Program and that of the Government of Ontario through the Ontario Media Development Corporation's Ontario Book Initiative. We further acknowledge the support of the Canada Council for the Arts and the Ontario Arts Council for our publishing program.

Typeset in Garamond by M&S, Toronto
Printed and Bound in the United States Of America
McClelland & Stewart Ltd.
75 Sherbourne Street
Toronto, Ontario
M5A 2P9
www.mcclelland.com/NCL
    2 3 4 5   12 11 10 09

AUTHOR'S NOTE

This story, the characters, and the names are all imaginary.
They have no known existence.

I have taken some liberties with topography, and with
the Thompson River, whose colour changes strikingly with the
seasons.

E.W.

Vancouver
British Columbia
June, 1946

"No man is an Iland, intire of it selfe; every man is a peece of the Continent, a part of the maine; if a Clod bee washed away by the Sea, Europe is the lesse, as well as if a Promontorie were, as well as if a Mannor of thy friends or of thine owne were; any mans death diminishes me, because I am involved in Mankinde;"

"And makes one little room an everywhere."

"Good is as visible as greene,"

JOHN DONNE

ONE

The day that Mrs. Dorval's furniture arrived in Lytton, Ernestine and I had gone to the station to see the train come in. It was a hot day. The heat of the sun burned down from above, it beat up from the ground and was reflected from the hot hills. Mr. Miles, the station agent, was in his shirt-sleeves; the station dog lay and panted, got up, moved away, lay down and panted again; and the usual Indians stood leaning against the corners of the wooden station (we called it "the deepo") in their usual curious incurious fashion, not looking as though they felt the heat or anything else. The Indians always looked as though they had nothing to do, and perhaps they had nothing to do. Ernestine and I had nothing much to do, but school was out and supper wasn't ready and so we had drifted over to the station. Neither of our mothers liked us to do this every day; but we were not absolutely forbidden.

When the train clanked in, a number of the stifling passengers got out seeking coolness in the bright glaring heat of the station platform. Ernestine and I watched these passengers with experienced eyes and saw that there was no one interesting to us. We did not find grown-ups interesting, but were always on the look-out for other children or for dogs. And sure enough there at the end of the train was a large dog, perhaps a Newfoundland, hot in his hot coat. The train men had got him out of a freight car, and then they heaved and pushed and lifted out a huge crated object that might be a piano, and then they got out packing case after packing case.

Directly the great dog stood upon the platform, looking sadly and nobly about him, a woman moved up to him and said casually, "Well, Sailor," and you might almost say the dog smiled. His thick bell-rope of a tail swung and he moved up to the woman who patted him lightly but gave her full attention to the crates and packing cases that the train hands and station hands deposited upon the platform. Ernestine and I had seen this woman before in the Lytton main street, but she was really the kind of woman that you don't notice. You might see her in a village, or in a big city, or in a street-car, or on a train, and you would never notice. Nevertheless, we now saw that she had authority. She was dressed in dark grey. Her hair was dark grey too, and was taken straight back from her plain strong face. Suddenly she began to be interesting to Ernestine and to me, because she belonged to Sailor the dog and to all the new packing cases.

We did not need to ask, because, before you could count fifty, word had travelled along the platform, perhaps from the station agent or perhaps from the express company, to us and through us, and even to the leaning inscrutable Indians, that the dog Sailor and all these packing cases belonged to a Mrs. Dorval and that Mrs. Dorval had taken that square bunga-low all alone above the river, just to the east of Lytton. So as Ernestine and I had nothing better to do, we trailed along the dusty road behind the waggon that took the first load out. The horses toiled up the winding trail, sending up clouds of fine clay dust, and we idled far enough behind to be out of the worst of it. Mrs. Dorval rode with the teamster. The trucks were out that day and one was broken down, so they had to use the team. The toiling waggon topped three or four little slopes before it reached the square bungalow above the river. Only the knowledge that we were to see something new in Lytton, and the niceness of having something to tell our families that would cause us to be important made Ernestine and me keep on walking in the dust and heat behind the waggon, because the declining sun, still just above the high near hills, was very hot indeed. You couldn't walk on the side of the road very well because there was nothing but sage and tumbleweed, and that made walking difficult, although it was easy enough to ride horseback there.

The sun dipped behind the hills across the river and the windows of the bungalow ceased blazing with evening sunlight. At once you felt the cool air as if it were the earth's cool breath. Anybody looking out of the front windows of Mrs. Dorval's bungalow could look down on to the racing Thompson River. Perhaps the water was emerald, perhaps it was sapphire. It is both. It is neither. It is a brilliant river, blue-green with lacings of white foam and spray as the water hurls itself violently along in rapids against hidden or projecting rocks, a rapid, racing, calling river. The hills rise high and lost on each side of the banks. These hills are traversed hardly at all. There is no reason to climb, to scale the top, to look down. In the sunlight the dun-coloured gorges of the blue-green river look yellow and ochreous, and in some places there are out-croppings of rock that are nearly rose red. Large dark and soli-tary pine trees give landmark and meaning. Here and there in a gully an army of these dark pointed pine trees marches up an ancient waterway of the hill-side, static. How do they grow on stone? A figure of man or of beast crawling distant across the great folds and crevasses of these sprawling hills would make you stop, look, point with surprise, and question. One is accustomed to their being empty of life. As evening comes on, the hills grow dove grey and purple; they take on a variety of surprising shapes and shades, and the oblique shafts of sunlight disclose new hills and valleys which in daylight merge into one and are not seen. It is the sage-brush that covers nearly everything, that helps to transform everything, and that in the mutations of sunlight and moonlight helps to change the known hills to the unfamiliar. Because the hills are so desolate, strange and still, without movement, the strong brilliant water in headlong motion at their base holds your eyes with its tumult. If the person in Mrs. Dorval's bungalow feels any fear of this desolate scene, or if the person is subject in solitude to moods of depression or despair, then that person had better take her piano and her dog Sailor and her packing cases and go by train or by the Cariboo highway to some comfortable town full of people. No one can travel by the Thompson River at Lytton; it is too turbulent and too thickly sown with rapids.

Ernestine and I stood and watched the woman in grey deal with the first waggon-load of furniture and belongings, and with a subsequent load. She dealt with the teamster and his helper with such speed and capableness that never at any moment was there that look of lost untidiness begotten of a welter of unrelated and unarranged objects. Ernestine and I began to admire this woman whom an hour or so ago we had neglected to notice. Time passed, the sky darkened, and lights appeared in the valley down by the Bridge. The dry noise of crickets became vociferous and imperative. I understood a tension in Ernestine, for we felt that our experience was not complete. We were going to be late for supper. We were due for a wigging when we got home, she from her mother, and I from our friend Mrs. Dunne with whom I was boarded. But Ernestine's mother and my Mrs. Dunne were both human, and if we arrived home with the account of words spoken and information gained, our distinction might atone. "Yes, my daughter was speaking to Mrs. Dorval only last evening!" Sailor ambled up and obligingly nosed our skinny legs. He was lovely. We were pleased and flattered; it was almost as if Mrs. Dorval herself had noticed us. We stooped and fondled him lavishly. Ernestine was not shy, so she led the trundling Sailor by his collar back to the woman in grey.

"Here is Sailor, Mrs. Dorval," she said.

The woman in grey did not stop to smile or thank Ernestine for her empty courtesy. She said without pausing, "All right. I am not Mrs. Dorval," and continued taking things into the house. It was rather humiliating that a small group of silent Indian children saw this happen. Charley Joe and Joe Charley and some of their brothers and sisters had stopped on their way to the rancheree farther up the river. They would stand there until there was nothing left to see, and then they would move slowly away, impelled one by the other. Goodness knows what they would tell the other Indians in their log and earth houses when they reached home. You never knew. Ernestine and I turned in the dusk, rather confused, and walked away until we passed the first crest and the road led downwards. Then we saw the lights of Lytton and together we started to run, and recovered ourselves. The river was dark now, but even in the darkness we saw the white wave crests curling and tumbling in the rapids near us as we ran, and the noise of the water was louder than ever in the darkness. The smell of the sage came strong.

ETHEL WILSON

I felt sorrier for Ernestine than for myself because no one likes to be snubbed. And she loved dogs so dearly that when she was fifteen she waded into the Fraser River just below the Bridge, and swam out a few strokes to save a little dog, and was carried away by the current and was drowned. It was terrible. The little dog was drowned too.

6

TWO

Every town that stands at a confluence of rivers has something over and above other towns. This is true whether the town is little or big. Lytton was so small that relatively it was a village. But relative to the surrounding solitudes it was a town. Roads converged there. The railroad passed through it, trains stopped there, it was fed by this system and it fed the surrounding solitudes for a long radius, especially northwards into the hills.

But what gives Lytton its especial character, lying there at the fringe of the sage-brush carpet in a fold of the hills at the edge of the dry belt and the coast area, is that just beside the town the clear turbulent Thompson River joins the vaster opaque Fraser. The Fraser River, which begins as a sparkling stream in the far northern mountains, describes a huge curve in northern British Columbia, and, increased in volume by innumerable rills and streams and by large and important tributary rivers, grows in size and reputation and changes its character and colour on its journey south.

Long before the Fraser reaches Lytton it has cut its way through different soils and rocks and has taken to itself tons of silt, and now moves on, a wide deceptive flow of sullen opaque and fawn-coloured water. Evidences of boil and whirl-pool show the river to be dangerous. At Lytton it is refreshed and enlarged by the blue-green racing urgent Thompson River. This river in the course of its double journey from north and east spreads itself into lakes and gathers itself together again into a river, until as it approaches Lytton it manifests all its special beauty and brilliance.

At the point where the Thompson, flowing rapidly west-wards from Kamloops, pours itself into the Fraser, flowing widely and sullenly southwards from the Lillooet country, is the Bridge. The Bridge springs from a single strong gesture across the confluence of the rivers and feeds the roads and trails that lead into the northern hills which are covered with sage, and are dotted here and there with extravagantly noble pine trees. The way to my own home lay across the Bridge.

Ever since I could remember, it was my joy and the joy of all of us to stand on this strong iron bridge and look down at the line where the expanse of emerald and sapphire dancing water joins and is quite lost in the sullen Fraser. It is a mar-riage, where, as often in marriage, one overcomes the other, and one is lost in the other. The Fraser receives all the startling colour of the Thompson River and overcomes it, and flows on unchanged to look upon, but greater in size and quality than before. Ernestine and I used to say, "Let's go down to the Bridge," and there we would stand and lean on the railing and look down upon the hypnotizing waters. We would look up at the broad sweep of brown Fraser and the broad or steep banks curving northwards, at the small distant high fields of bright green alfalfa showing the work of man, and at the road following in hairpin curves the east bank of the river, leading up towards and beyond distant Lillooet. Then we would hear wheels or hooves and feel vibration on the bridge, and turn idly to see a conveyance creaking by driven by silent Indians. An old squaw drove, or a young boy, and the seats were piled with dark silent children brightly and darkly clad. Or perhaps a rancher driving in. We would turn and again look down at the bright water being lost in the brown, and as we talked and laid our little plans of vast importance for that day and the next, the sight of the cleaving joining waters and the sound of their never-ending roar and the feel of the frequent Lytton wind that blew down the channels of both the rivers were part and parcel of us, and conditioned, as they say, our feeling.

My family did not live in Lytton. Our ranch was about fifteen miles out of town as you turned off the winding road that led north following the course of the Fraser to and beyond Lillooet. We raised stock and alfalfa and some other kinds of feed, we had some dairy cows, and we had a water-wheel near the house with abundant water always, and that made it easier for us to live nicely. It made it easier, too, for us to keep chickens, a few hundred, and to have an excellent kitchen garden and an orchard. The irrigation, once set in motion, almost looked after itself. But my father and mother had a hard and hard-working life, just the same. When they were lucky, my father kept two hired men and more of course in summer and my mother kept a good girl in the house; but even then they worked hard from morning till night with little respite. According to economic conditions in the big outside world, ripples spread into this hinterland in the sage-brush, and therefore one hired man left after the other to better himself at the Coast, the girl went down to Vancouver to work in a restaurant, and my mother and father were left to cope as best they could with the uncertain help of nearby Indians. They had established a claim, years before, on the families of

Charley Joe and Joe Charley at the rancheree near Lytton, and these unpredictable and uncapable youths came and went. And then perhaps some hired help came back again.

I had no particular pride in the industry and gallantry of my parents. I took it for granted. Both Father and Mother set and maintained the family standards in an exacting loneliness where it would have been easy to be slipshod and lazy and soon engulfed in broken fences, unclean outhouses, dingy walls and curtains, and the everlasting always waiting encroachment of the sage-brush. But my ridiculous pride was that my mother had been at the Sorbonne. What the Sorbonne signified I did not quite know, but I knew that my mother had, through this Sorbonne-ness, perhaps, a quality that other women known to me did not possess. Mother had not told me about the Sorbonne, although she seemed to know about Paris. Mrs. Dunne in Lytton had told me. She said, "I always think it is so wonderful of a woman like your mother, who's been at the Sorbonne . . ." So then I asked Mother, and she told me a lot. Life, for me, could not have been bettered, what with the ranch, and such parents as mine, excursions into regions fed by books, my pony Maxey and the dogs, the rides into Lytton, and my friendships with Ernestine and the other Lytton children.

I suppose that Mother and Father debated more than I knew, but the result was that when I was old enough to ride the fifteen miles on Maxey alone (and we all knew the familiar road and country like the flat of our hands) I was sent to board with Mrs. Dunne in Lytton. I rode in on Sunday afternoons and went straight to Mrs. Dunne's, or over to Ernestine's, or if it was church-time and there was a service I tied Maxey to a fence post, beside other waiting horses, loosened his saddle a bit, and slipped into church, sitting wherever

I chose. People were always friendly; there was always a beck-
oning finger and a nod that meant "Sit here with us." Then
during the week I went to the public school, and twice a
week I went after school to the small Convent-Hospital west
of Lytton where there was a nun from Paris; she taught me
French, both talking and out of a book. The book was called
Chardenal and was useful, but the hour's talk with Sister
Marie-Cécile was good French and good discipline. Sister
Marie-Cécile hoped, I think, that she might gently win me to
Paradise, but I was a wary and stubborn young Protestant.
These hours at the Convent were the direct if long-delayed
result of the Sorbonne. On Friday afternoon I would saddle
Maxey, who ate his head off at Mr. Rossignol's stable most of
the week, and ride back to the ranch, bearing home all the
school news, town news, church news, store news, and carry-
ing special orders or presents tied to the horn of my saddle or
in a good roll behind me. Maxey was, of course, bridle-wise.
It was a lovely ride home, as you can imagine, all along the
Lillooet road, reining off into the sage-brush if a car came
along in a cloud of dust, and always with accustomed country
eyes roving the expanse that unfolded itself at each bend of
the river and road, noting whose cattle those were yonder, the
promenading hawks, in spring the bluebirds, in summer the
ground-hogs changing suddenly from little vertical statues to
scurrying dust-coloured vanishing points; in autumn reining
in and standing still to watch a flying crying skein of wild
geese, sometimes a coyote at close range – quite a pretty little
beast. And then at the end of the ride the dogs barking a
welcome, and Mother and Father and hugs, Maxey to be
stabled and fed, and a great big supper ready.

On the Friday after Ernestine and I had watched the set-
tling in of Mrs. Dorval – if it *was* Mrs. Dorval or had we

dreamed the name? – I told Father and Mother all that I knew and of course they were interested because a newcomer in a place the size of Lytton or in the sparsely settled neighbourhood was real news. I had learned just a little more, because Ernestine's father had a law office in Lytton and he must have known something about Mrs. Dorval coming, because he was trying to get a lady's saddle horse and perhaps another saddle horse too; he was trying through Mr. Rossignol who had the livery stable and the truck, and Mr. Rossignol said he might have to go as far as Guichon's up at Quilchena beyond Merritt before he could get just exactly the kind of horses that Ernestine's father wanted for Mrs. Dorval. This, in a horse country, made Mrs. Dorval more interesting than ever.

Following the small snub which the very much occupied woman who was not Mrs. Dorval had given to Ernestine and through Ernestine to me, we affected not to be very much interested in the new household. We did not go up again to the bungalow. There was nothing to take us up there as it was on the way to nowhere, and those children who had been up reported nothing except that there were curtains with flowers on in some of the windows, that Charley Joe and Joe Charley were working in the garden and mending the little fence, and that they seemed to be working hard. We saw the woman who was not Mrs. Dorval once or twice in Mattson's grocery store, where she gave quite large orders. But Mr. Mattson's impression was that she ordered all kinds of things from the stores in Vancouver, and it is true that many, many parcels of all sizes arrived by express. Ernestine's mother extorted from Ernestine's father the fact that the name of the woman in the grey dress was certainly not Mrs. Dorval. It was Mrs. Broom, which somehow changed her.

THREE

I t must have been September, and late September at that on account of what I saw that day when I was riding back to Lytton from the ranch. This time I had stayed at home only over Friday night, as Ernestine's cousins were coming down from Ashcroft early on the Sunday. There were two boys and a girl and their father and mother. We were going to have an all-day picnic up the river, and the fathers were going to do a little fishing. You could fish all day in the Thompson rapids, dropping your fly or a grasshopper just behind a large rock where the green water was for a moment still, and you thought there was a chance of a fish lurking and getting its wind back, if fishes do, but you would not get a strike. Nothing but the tug tug of the current as your fly drifted down. But there were some other spots near Lytton where the river made pools and the fishing was often good. It was the pleasantest thing you could think of, there in the shade of a clump of bushes, with the expectation of a good picnic lunch, or lying comfortably full of food, and watching Ernestine's father and uncle casting and casting, or just letting their lines sink. I liked Ernestine's cousins, too, and we always had a good time. It was an excitement whenever one of those picnics was planned, and I always came in from the ranch a day earlier so as not to miss it. It happened therefore that I was riding back on a Saturday afternoon instead of Sunday, quite late because I had stretched out my Saturday at home until Mother said I really must start or it would be dark when I got to Lytton. Mother and Father were not nervous at all about me and my long ride in, but Mother had a strong feeling about my not being out alone after dark. Mrs. Dunne was very careful about this too, and Mother had no misgivings once I was in Lytton.

I remember that Mother made me take my old buckskin jacket with the fringed edges in case it was nippy that evening, because the weather had just turned colder. When I first got that jacket it was a beauty. It had been made by the Indians up at Lillooet, and Father had got me the prettiest he could find, with beads in a pattern of deer, and plenty of fringe. If anyone ever adored a garment, I adored my buckskin jacket. It had grown a little small for me and quite dirty, but Mother laughed and said that gave it style. We all had buckskin jackets.

I must have ridden about ten miles or so, and was just rounding the corner of a bluff when I saw another rider, coming down the hill amongst the sage-brush. I had never seen the horse before; it was a beautiful horse. And certainly I had never seen the rider; indeed, you wouldn't see anyone like her in all our part of that western country. She seemed to be young and she had a good seat. She rode on one of those small English saddles – which other people didn't – and sat erect but easy; and no one near us wore that kind of riding clothes. It came to me with a hop, skip and a jump that this must be Mrs. Dorval and that must be the horse that Mr. Rossignol had been trying to get, up Quilchena way. If I kept on at my pace – I was loping along easily – and if Mrs. Dorval kept on riding carefully and slowly down the sage-dotted hill-side, we should just meet on the road. I felt very awkward, remembering the snub that Ernestine and I got at the bungalow, and I thought, "Now if Mrs. Dorval is snubby like Mrs. Broom this is going to be terrible, because I've had no experience and I don't know what to do." And although it was quite exciting to see Mrs. Dorval, because I had no doubt but that this was she, I would rather have had a grown-up with me, who would have known what to say and whether to go on or to drop behind or what. I slowed Maxey to a walk and hoped to goodness that Mrs. Dorval wouldn't even see me and that she would go on by herself in front of me all the way to Lytton. But that was absurd, because no rider could possibly help seeing another rider in all that solitude.

So it came that Mrs. Dorval, if it were she, reached the road first, and I had the opportunity of seeing how young she looked, and pretty, too, with a yellow shirt and a soft felt hat, and riding breeches; and how neatly she handled the beautiful mare. She turned in her saddle and waited, looking at me. She must have seen a small figure of the country in a shabby buckskin jacket, riding a pony which could have done with a bit of grooming.

When I came up close to Mrs. Dorval I saw only that her face was very pretty as she smiled gently at me, and so I smiled back, I suppose.

Mrs. Dorval said to me in a very light voice, "Are you riding in to Lytton?" and I said, "Yes."

Then she said, "What a nice pony, is he yours?" and I said, "Yes."

And then she said, as we started walking our horses together as though it were taken for granted that we should, "What is your name, little girl?"

Now I would have resented "little girl," for I was twelve, if it had not been said in that light soft voice of Mrs. Dorval's. So I said, "My name is Frankie, at least Frances Burnaby," and then I added, "Mrs. Dorval."

Mrs. Dorval turned to me with that brilliant expression that I learned to know and said, "How did you know my name?"

I was much too shy to explain that of course everyone in Lytton and for miles round knew her name even if they hadn't seen her, and that they would know her the minute they saw her; that they knew she "had money," and had two horses, and a big black dog called Sailor, and lived in the square bungalow standing alone east of Lytton; that a Mrs. Broom lived with her and seemed to do the work, and that Mrs. Dorval never came into Lytton, but that Mrs. Broom did the shopping. I could have told her that people in houses, and on verandahs, and in bedrooms, and in stores, and in stables, asked each other if they knew whether Mrs. Dorval had a husband, and was he dead, and why had she come here? This all swept through my mind, but was so impossible to tell her, that I only stammered, "Oh, I thought you must be."

We walked our horses side by side, I feeling at the same time diffident and important. Mrs. Dorval did not "make conversation." I discovered that she never did. It began to seem so easy and natural riding beside her there and no one making an effort at conversation that I was able to steal a few looks at her side face. This was especially easy because she hardly seemed to know that I was beside her; she just took me for granted in a natural fashion. Through the years in the various times and places in which I came to know Mrs. Dorval, I never failed to have the same faint shock of delight as I saw her profile in repose, as it nearly always was. I can only describe it by saying that it was very pure. Pure is perhaps the best word, or spiritual, shall I say, and I came to think that what gave her profile this touching purity was just the soft curve of her high cheekbone, and the faint hollow below it. Also the innocence of her slightly tilted nose, which afterwards I called in my mind a flirt's nose, and the slight droop of her mouth whose upper lip was perhaps a little over-full.

We rode along the dusty highway which had a series of hairpin turns at the edge of deep dusty sage-dotted gullies, and this made the distance to Lytton much longer than as the crow flies. We came out on the point of one of the hairpin turns and my ears, which were used to country silences and sounds, heard that sound that will thrill me till I die. I reined Maxey in at once, and, quite forgetting the importance of Mrs. Dorval, pointed up and said, "Look!"

Mrs. Dorval reined in too, and said, "What? Where?" She shaded her eyes with her hand and looked up as I did. She could not see as quickly as I could that out of the north came a thin long arrow, high in the sky. Then her eyes picked up the movement of the fluid arrow rapidly approaching overhead, and the musical clamour of the wild geese came more clearly and loudly to us. The valley of the Fraser lay broad below, lit by the September afternoon, and the geese, not too high, were now nearly overhead, travelling fast. The fluid arrow was an acute angle wavering and changing, one line straggling out far behind the other. It cleft the skies, and as always I felt an exultation, an uprush within me joining that swiftly moving company and that loud music of the wild geese. As we gazed, the moving arrow of great birds passed out of sight on its known way to the south, leaving only the memory of sight and sound in the still air. We drew a long breath.

"*God*," said Mrs. Dorval. Then, "What a sight!"

I was brought shockingly to earth. I was quite used to hearing the men round Mr. Rossignol's stable, and other men too, say "God" for no reason at all. And it goes without saying that the Rev. Mr. Thompson said "God" in church, as it were officially, and that we all sang about God with nothing more than ordinary church-going emotion. But never, never, in our house (except once or twice, Father) or in Ernestine's house or at Mrs. Dunne's or in any of our friends' houses (unless we were saying our prayers) did people ever mention God. It would have seemed an unnatural thing to do, which, come to think of it, is strange. So when I heard Mrs. Dorval say "*God*" in that way, it took her out of the likelihood of Mrs. Dunne's house or Ernestine's mother's, and probably out of the church, and somehow peculiarly connected her with Mr. Rossignol's stable.

We remained standing there and gazing at the empty sky. Then Mrs. Dorval turned her face on me and I realized all of a sudden that she had another face. This full face was different from the profile I had been studying, and was for the moment animated. Her brows, darker than her fair hair, pointed slightly upwards in the middle in moments of stress and became in appearance tragic, and her eyes which were fringed with thick, short, dark lashes opened wide and looked brilliant instead of serene. The emotion might be caused by pain, by the beauty of fighting geese, by death, or even by some very mild physical discomfort, but the impact on the beholder was the same, and arresting. Ordinarily, Mrs. Dorval's full face was calm and somewhat indolent. The purity was not there, but there was what I later came to regard as a rather pleasing yet disturbing sensual look, caused I think by the over-fullness of the curved mouth, and by those same rounded high cheekbones which in profile looked so tender. Whatever it was, it is a fact that the side face and the full face gave not the same impression, but that both had a rapt striking beauty when her eyebrows showed distress.

"Can we often see that?" she asked. "Will it ever come again? Oh Frankie, when we stood there and the geese went over, we didn't seem to be in our bodies at all, did we? And I seemed to be up with them where I'd really love to be. Did you feel like that?"

That was so exactly how the wild geese always made me feel, that I was amazed. Perhaps Mother and Father felt like that because they, too, dearly loved watching the geese passing overhead, but somehow we would never *never* have said that to each other – it would have made us all feel uncomfortable. But Mrs. Dorval said it naturally, and was not at all uncomfortable, and it gave me a great deal of pleasure to agree with her without confusion and apology.

We began to ride on, talking from time to time, and when we got to the Lytton Bridge, Mrs. Dorval said, "I'm starving, aren't you? Come home with me and Mouse will give us some tea."

This was more than I could ever have hoped for, and I did not see that there could be any harm, so I said, "Oh thank you, I'd love to," feeling very much pleased and impressed. We stopped our horses for a minute on the Bridge, and looked down at the bright water hurrying to be lost in the brown and at the moving line where the one entered the other. Then on the far side of the Bridge we turned up to the left. It happened that as we rode to Mrs. Dorval's bungalow to have tea we met no one.

When we topped the third slope Sailor came to meet us, barking and wagging and cavorting in his own large way. Mrs. Dorval dismounted and bent to pat Sailor. She called out in that light voice, "Tea, Mouse, we're starving! Lots of toast and jam!" and I slid down off Maxey and threw the reins forward over his head. Maxey was very safe that way. Slide the reins over his head and he'd never go away. We went round and stabled Mrs. Dorval's mare and then we went into the house.

I am not going to describe the house inside because I have seen plenty of houses since, and so has everyone, that are as charming. But it was a revelation to me then, in comfort and colour; so was the little grand piano, and so were the queerly painted book-shelves. Mrs. Broom came to the door of the living-room from the kitchen, I supposed, and gave me a look, and then went back and I heard tea noises. Mrs. Dorval began to ask me about my buckskin jacket, so I told her, and I said, "They make them in white too, and gauntlets for riding; they're lovely and soft but they're very expensive."

"Mouse, do you hear that?" called Mrs. Dorval to the kitchen. "You must order a white buckskin jacket and gloves for me at once. They would be too divine." I had not heard people say "too divine" before. We didn't talk like that.

When the tea came in there was tea and toast and jam in a bowl and a fruit cake, not icing cake like we always had. Mrs. Dorval prodded the jam with the spoon. "Something out of a tin," she said with a little disgust, and she passed it to me. "Have some glue." When I had helped myself politely I thought it was very nice jam. I decided that Mrs. Dorval must be used to very exalted jam, and admired her all the more even for this.

We were having a lovely time, at least I was, when I looked out of the window and saw the Rev. Mr. Thompson standing at the top of the slope approaching the bungalow as if he were a little puffed with all that climbing. While he was getting his breath he stood and looked at the broad high view.

"Excuse me, Mrs. Dorval," I said, "but there's Mr. Thompson."

"Who," said Mrs. Dorval, "is Mr. Thompson and where is he?"

"He's our minister, *there*," I said, pointing.

Mrs. Dorval looked out of the window. Her face was brilliant with tragedy. "Mouse," she called in agitation, "do something! Send him away! Give him ten dollars, or fifteen – give him anything – he's come to collect! I don't want him!"

Mrs. Broom came out of the kitchen and looked almost with distaste at Mrs. Dorval. "Sit down and don't be childish," she said, "he's only come to pay you a call."

"But I don't *want* a call!" said Mrs. Dorval with a surprised air, but still in her unhurried way. "I don't want *any* calls." She looked at me. "I think," she said, "it would be better if you slipped into the bedroom because I *don't* want him to think I'm having callers."

This all seemed very queer to me, but I did as I was told and went into the bedroom with my cup of tea and sat down rather behind the door but where I could see Mrs. Dorval. Evidently Mrs. Broom let Mr. Thompson in and then she went back to the kitchen. Next I saw Mrs. Dorval get up and hold out her hand in a trustful way just as though she had been wanting Mr. Thompson to come and see her very much indeed. I couldn't hear what they said at first as they were moving about and then sitting down; but after that I couldn't help hearing every word, and I could still see Mrs. Dorval but not Mr. Thompson.

"Then you are English," continued Mr. Thompson.

"Well . . . no," said Mrs. Dorval.

"Is your husband English? Or I should say, was your home there?"

"No," said Mrs. Dorval.

There was a pause.

"I hope your husband will be able to join you here," said Mr. Thompson.

"Oh, I *do* hope so," said Mrs. Dorval. She spoke little, but her words did not come snubbingly as Mrs. Broom's would have done, but gently.

"A reader, I see," said Mr. Thompson.

"Yes," said Mrs. Dorval.

Mr. Thompson got up and evidently went over to the book-shelves where I had seen a lot of yellowish paper books.

"Ah, you read French!"

"Yes, I read French."

"I should like you to meet my wife. She would be very glad to call upon you, she is a reader too."

"Call?" said Mrs. Dorval vaguely and sweetly. "Oh, not call, you have no idea . . . Oh, you are so kind, but at present . . ." and she looked tenderly at Mr. Thompson.

Mr. Thompson murmured something about "restored health" and then after a little more unsatisfactory conversation, said what I had been waiting for him to say, "And now shall we have a word of prayer?"

"Oh," breathed Mrs. Dorval, sitting motionless.

I knew what Mr. Thompson was doing. I had seen it many times. When Mr. Thompson said, "And now shall we have a word of prayer?" all of us who were assembled in the room rose, turned round, dropped upon our knees, put our elbows on our chair seats, folded our hands, and closed our eyes. Mr. Thompson did the same. Then he prayed out loud. We didn't like doing it very much but we all liked Mr. Thompson, so of course we did it.

Mrs. Dorval sat motionless and then said, "Do I have to

do that too, or would it be all right if I just did this?" and she clasped her hands and closed her eyes and looked like a saint in ecstasy.

Mr. Thompson in process of getting down on his knees mumbled that that would be all right. There was a silence and then Mr. Thompson said slowly, with pauses, in a sincere and special voice, "Our Dear Heavenly Father, we thank Thee for Thy goodness to us in this our pilgrimage on earth. Thou knowest each of us though we are strangers to one another. Thou knowest our secret hearts, our troubles and our joys. Do, we pray Thee, bless these Thy servants. Keep in our hearts our love to Thee and our love to one another. Bless, our Dear Father, those who live within this house and make them a blessing. We ask this all in the name of Thy Dear Son our Lord." (I had heard this good prayer before and nearly knew it.) Then Mr. Thompson said the Lord's Prayer, but he said it alone. There was stillness and a pause in the room.

When after this silence Mr. Thompson rose to his feet, Mrs. Dorval opened her eyes. "Oh, that was beautiful!" she murmured, looking up at Mr. Thompson. "Did you really mean that, Mr. Thompson? It was so kind to ask a blessing on us! I don't know when I've been so touched. I do appreciate it, so very much." And she stood up to say good-bye. The room seemed full of understanding.

"I don't know what church you belong to, Mrs. Dorval," said Mr. Thompson kindly, "but I'm very sure we'd all be glad to see you on Sunday."

"Oh, I don't go to church," said Mrs. Dorval in her unhurried way, "but Mouse goes. She loves going to church, don't you, Mouse? Where are you? . . . I'll tell her about it. Mouse will be sure to come." Mrs. Dorval's light easy way relegated church to something which infinitely did not matter.

"Oh, are you going?" gently. "That was a most beautiful prayer you made for us, Mr. Thompson. How very kind of you to come!" And then with a little gush of friendliness to the departing Mr. Thompson, "*Good*-bye!"

I admired Mrs. Dorval's disposal of Mr. Thompson; yet there was something somewhere that was not quite right.

I heard the front door close, and Mrs. Dorval opened wide the bedroom door, without any comment to me. I came out and saw Mr. Thompson going down the hill in the dusk. I think now that there was a burning sort of goodness and directness in Mr. Thompson against which Mrs. Dorval had had to defend herself with her weapon of lightness.

Mrs. Broom came in to take away the tea things. "Now Mouse," said Mrs. Dorval, "I will not be called upon. I will not have my life complicated here . . . people coming in like this! I do not propose to spend my time paying attention to all kinds of people. You know perfectly well that I can't have people running in, and you must stop it." (It might have been Mrs. Broom's fault.) "All I ask of anybody is to be left alone and not be interfered with. I'm sure I always leave people quite alone and interfere with nobody."

"*You!*" said Mrs. Broom with a peculiar intonation. And she gave a short little laugh that sounded to me like "Ha!" as she went out with the tea things.

Mrs. Dorval was quite serene now that she had handed Mr. Thompson and the population of Lytton over to Mrs. Broom. She took off her hat and tossed it on to the couch. Then she went to the piano and began to play. I sat still and bolt upright.

She turned to me. "Do you like singing?" she asked, and without waiting for an answer, she began to sing.

"Drink to me only with thine eyes
And I will pledge with mine . . ."

This old song was new to me, but the simple repeated phrases within their small compass of notes made the tune familiar before it died away.

"Oh . . ." I began, but she went on as if I were not there.

"There is a Lady sweet and kind,
Was never face so pleas'd my mind;
I did but see her passing by,
And yet I love her till I die."

("Why, that's Mrs. Dorval her very own self!" I thought, bedazzled.) And then she sang some comical-sounding French songs. They made me laugh, though I couldn't understand them. She had a sweet, true voice, and strong, although for the most part she sang softly. You could see that she loved singing. As for me, a country child, I had come under a very fancy kind of spell, near to infatuation.

She stopped. I felt suddenly that I had stayed too long, and said so. She came with me to the door and told me to be sure to come and have tea with her again, and of course I said "Yes" ardently. I was very happy because she seemed to like me.

"But," she said slowly, "perhaps you'd better not tell other people that you've been. If they know that you come they'll all come – calls, calls, calls, and I don't want them, I can't bear it – no, don't say a word to anyone, will you, Frankie? Promise! Save, me, won't you?"

Whatever she had asked me, then, I would have agreed to do, and this seemed a small thing to promise, so I did. But it passed through my mind that it would be a funny thing if I came to this house and my mother couldn't come, that is, even if she wanted to. But I was only twelve, and was under a novel spell of beauty and singing and the excitement of a charm that was new, and I went away almost in a trance. As I mounted Maxey I caught sight of Mouse standing in the doorway a step above Mrs. Dorval, who gave a wave of farewell.

"Keeping your hand in, I see, Hester," said Mouse disagreeably and quite loudly.

"Don't be ridiculous, Mouse," said Mrs. Dorval, and went inside.

As I rode down the hill I tried to collect my impressions. Through all the surprise and delight ran a mean little disturbing thought. I was to tell no one of my visit. Not Mother and Father?

I did not tell Ernestine or anyone in Lytton, and nearly a week had passed before I was at the ranch again and by that time I had become used to the idea of not telling.

FOUR

F ollowing my first visit to Hester Dorval I had an existence that was not natural for a child. While I lived my life in the accustomed routine of school and of visits home to the ranch each week, I, who had never had secrets, was possessed by two desires which were secret. One was not to disclose by any slip of speech my acquaintance with Mrs. Dorval lest I should embarrass or disturb her, and the other desire was that I should in some way see her again and could accept the invitation to come and have tea with her. Everything turned on these things. But I lived in a glass goldfish bowl where the behaviour of each fish was visible to all the other fishes, and also to grown-up people outside and in the vicinity of the glass bowl. So I took to being very secretive indeed, with myself at all events, and possibly Ernestine may have noticed this too. I was not as happy as I had always been, and yet I was happier, because I had something exciting waiting always round the corner. Several times when I went home I was on the brink of telling Father and Mother about my chance meeting and my visit, and yet I always stopped, because much as I admired Mrs. Dorval I was un-sentimental enough to realize that there was something silly and unreasonable in her exaction of a promise from me that I should not tell that I had been to see her, and I would rather not reveal this to my parents, promise or no, lest they should find her ridiculous. And then there was this – they might for some unknown grown-up reason stop me going to the bungalow.

It could not be expected of a child of twelve that she should recognize in the space of an afternoon the complete self-indulgence and idleness of a new and charming friend, but there is no question now about the self-indulgence and idleness of Hetty. She was capable of kindness and consideration as long as her comfort was not in any way disturbed. If any person or any thing threatened her comfort or her desires, then that person or thing no longer existed as far as she was concerned, and such a person or such a thing was for her exactly as though he, she, or it had never been. Mrs. Broom must have known this for a long time. I had seen Mrs. Broom's strange attitude of devotion to and criticism of her employer in that one short afternoon, and I could not help wondering about it. I thought perhaps Mrs. Broom was some relative of Mrs. Dorval's, but then it did not seem likely that Mrs. Dorval would keep her relative in the kitchen. Civilized men and animals have, we see, a different moral and sexual code. And again amongst animals the code varies. The wild goose, for example, a moral bird, and the domestic promiscuous cat, appear to have entirely different values. Why this is so, is puzzling. Mr. and Mrs. Goose, they say, but not Mr. and Mrs. Cat. Hetty Dorval was a human cat in some ways, and yet cats have sometimes malice, and they sharpen their claws. But Hetty had no malice. She was as incapable of bearing malice as of bearing resentment. She simply shed people, and I only once caught a glimpse of her claws.

I saw her once or twice during my rides out and in, and she seemed indifferent but on the whole pleased to see me. During that winter I managed two or three times to go up to the bungalow, by some manoeuvring and by some hoodwinking of Mrs. Dunne and also of Ernestine, which did not raise me in my own estimation. The first time it was dark but not late, because of course it got dark very early in winter amidst the high hills – and I ran up the last slope and saw the lights in the bungalow windows where no curtains were drawn. There were no passers-by and there was no need to draw the curtains. I saw as I passed the window on the way to the front door that Mrs. Dorval sat at the piano singing. She was wearing what I suppose was a tea-gown or negligée sort of dress of light blue. I had never seen anything of that kind before, and she looked to my eyes like a princess. Mrs. Broom sat sewing. This woman was formidable to me and I was sorry to see her in the room. I listened and looked during two or three songs and then when Mrs. Dorval dropped her hands to her knees and turned and spoke to Mrs. Broom I summoned up my courage and darted to the door and knocked.

Mrs. Broom opened the door, looked at me and turned, and spoke over her shoulder to Mrs. Dorval. Then she told me to come in, and I was aware that she picked up her sewing and went at once to the kitchen.

"Frankie! Frankie Burnaby!" said Mrs. Dorval with delight and with a welcome in her tone and in her face, "why haven't you been to see me again? I've been looking and looking for you! You mustn't neglect me like this!" Neglect her!

I glowed with pleasure and I believed her words and the tone of her voice and her gentle welcoming smile; and it wasn't till afterwards that I thought that a woman as clever as Mrs. Dorval, who could read French, play the piano all up and down the keys and sing, and ride too, would surely know that she herself had put me, by virtue of my promise, into a difficult position that prevented my coming to see her with any ease or frankness, and that she had put me in a very deceiving position with my elders too. With my parents, for instance. The reason was that nobody existed for her as an individual who had ties or responsibilities and a life of his or her own. People only existed when they came within her vision. Beyond that she had neither care nor interest. She took me by my hands. "You're *cold!*" she said compassionately, and drew me to the fire. She went to the kitchen door, and I admired the way her long blue gown swept the floor, and the way that the long open sleeves fell loose from her arms and hands. She called, "Mouse, here's Frankie Burnaby freezing to death. Make us some cocoa, will you?"

When she came back to the fireplace she curled up on the couch and looked at me so kindly that I wondered why I had not somehow broken through and come before and settled down again to this warm pleasure. However, I had come prepared to ask a question which had been puzzling me, and this I did at once while I remembered.

"Mrs. Dorval," I said, "is Mrs. Broom your aunty?"

"My aunty?" said Hetty, her eyebrows pointing up in surprise. "No, she's no relation at all. What makes you think so? But she's all the parents I've ever had. My father and mother died in China. I don't remember them, but Mouse was my Nanny and she's stayed with me always. She doesn't approve of me but she spoils me and I couldn't do without her. And I don't believe Mouse could do without me, either. When I was at the Convent, Mouse was always near and looked after me in the holidays. My parents had arranged that," she said vaguely.

How romantic! China. An orphan. The Convent. And

here we were sitting by the fire in Lytton and Mouse bringing in the cocoa; and after the cocoa Hetty played and sang again. It was the most wonderful evening I had ever spent in my life. She did not press me to stay, and I had a feeling when I left that it was a matter of indifference to her whether I stayed or went, for of course the presence of an admiring child could not have been much of a diversion for her. I'm sure I had begun to bore her. But I would go again.

I spent two or three evenings like that. I longed to tell Father and Mother, and yet I was so far embarked and involved that I feared to do it, and trusted to luck that somehow it would be all right. So I kept quiet. And then one day in spring Ernestine said to me, "Did you know that Mr. Dorval came today?"

I said stupidly, "*Mr.* Dorval?" By this time I had forgotten that probably Hester Dorval was not living entirely in a vacuum and that there must be some reason for her existence in Lytton, and things that I did not know. "Have you seen him?" I asked.

"No," said Ernestine, "but Billy Miles was down at the train when he came in, and he had lovely suitcases and he went right away up to the bungalow. He's tall."

"Is he nice?" I asked anxiously.

"I don't know whether he's nice or not," said Ernestine.

Talk had begun again in the town about Mrs. Dorval and about her husband. Everyone happened to mention that he had come, but no one knew anything. Even my parents said casually they had heard that a Mr. Dorval had come to town. Had I seen him? I said, "No," which was true.

But a few days later, Ernestine, standing beside me on the Bridge and looking down at the rushing water, said, "What do you say, Frankie, if we go up to the bungalow some night and look in at the window? He's got the big black horse up there that Mr. Rossignol's been keeping down at the stable, and Mr. Rossignol says they go riding every day but they never come into town, and next thing he'll be gone and we'll never have seen him. What say, Frankie?"

I jumped at the idea, because I was dying with curiosity to see what Hester Dorval's husband would be like, and I was longing to see into the living-room again. If I went with Ernestine I didn't have to tell her I'd ever been there before. Ernestine had seen Mrs. Dorval, but only at a distance, and she was terribly curious. She had planned this because her parents were going to the skating rink for a meeting that night. Mrs. Dunne would be going too, so it would be easy for us to get away.

When our elders were well on their way, Ernestine and I met, and walked through the lovely spring evening, still dark, up the hills between the sage that smelled so much stronger at night, or perhaps one noticed it more. When the lights showed in the bungalow we slowed up and became a little more stealthy and crept along till we reached the lighted windows. We felt rather mean, but excited.

We tiptoed up to a window, and saw the live firelight playing on the room, and a lighted lamp or two. Mrs. Dorval was curled up on the couch as usual, and the lamplight fell upon her face. We had to be very careful, for her eyes were towards us, and her look might mean anything. She was watching with her tender happy smile a big man in the arm-chair, whose back was towards us. He was talking, and by the puffs that we saw, he was smoking a pipe. Hetty listened to him, and it looked as if she were following with indolent fond attention everything he said. Each word. Each look. No one but he in the room. No one but he in the world.

The man moved in his chair and got up. He moved to the fireplace, standing with his back to it and ramming the tobacco down his pipe with a match. He looked down at Hetty and went on talking, and Hetty lifted her head. The lamplight and the firelight shone on her face as she looked up at him.

We were able now to see something of Mr. Dorval's face. He was heavily built and he carried his head thrust forward so that there was a sense of power about him. Although his face was heavy, his look was alert and intent. When, as rarely, Hetty spoke, he jerked his head forward a little as if to listen and to seize the full value of her words. Once, laughing, she raised her hand to him, and he took it, and held it, and continued talking, looking down upon her.

We stayed watching until I felt a little pinch from Ernestine that I took to mean we'd better get away. I felt too, that this eavesdropping business was not very nice and I don't think we thought much of ourselves, doing it, except that it was fun in a way. I took another good look at Mr. Dorval, and of course I shall never forget his face, although I never saw him again; but I heard, afterwards, that he came to Lytton two or three times. I saw his picture in a newspaper some time later, and the name under the picture was not Dorval.

All this winter and spring there had been much talk at the ranch of my going away to boarding-school. It was exciting, but I did not know whether to be glad or sorry. Father and Mother had planned always that I should some day have a year or two in England, or perhaps in France, like Mother, and they had saved and probably denied themselves a great deal with this in mind. Now although I had my French lessons each week with Sister Marie-Cécile, there were other school subjects that Mother and Father said I would be behind in if I went straight from Lytton to England, and their plan was that

I should go to a school in Vancouver when I was about fourteen (I was thirteen by this time), and have some special teaching so that I should not find myself too unequal when I arrived at a strange school. It had practically been decided that I should go to Vancouver in the following spring, that is, in a year's time. And then one or two things happened to change this.

Father had bought another five acres north of the ranch house and this necessitated some more fencing, and he got Joe Charley and Charley Joe, who always travelled together, to come up from Lytton and help with this work. Partly they fed themselves, but partly we fed them, and they used to come to the kitchen a good deal, and Mother or Jean would give them fresh meat, or milk, or a baking of bread.

One Friday evening I rode up to the ranch and saw no one about, so I slid off Maxey and stabled him and ran into the house. Mother was in the kitchen and I rushed up and kissed her. She did not respond in her usual way and I felt that there was something wrong. Mother looked at me for a minute as if she were reading or learning me off by heart and she was rather quiet. My guilty conscience stirred, but I had carried on my peculiar occasional secret friendship with Hetty Dorval for so many months that I did not at once think about that. I said, "Where's Father?" and Mother said, "I don't know." That's all she said. I stayed in the kitchen a minute or two, but then as Mother did not seem to have anything more to say I wandered out to the corral. Father was there with a bunch of work horses we had. I called to him, and he looked up quickly and gave me a wave of the hand and went on with what he was doing. I felt uneasy, as ordinarily Father would have hailed me and beckoned me over to the corral, or I would have gone without being beckoned, and would have wriggled inside or climbed up on the stockade and leaned over. But Father did not seem to encourage me to do this. When things are not right one sometimes avoids contacts, as the easy natural words do not come.

So I went back and up to my room, and looked at things, and then went down to the kitchen again. Soon it was supper-time and Father came in and washed, and we all sat down at the table in the living-room.

Father and Mother were very polite to me, and I realized later that they wanted to get supper over and let me enjoy my meal first if possible before they said to me what was on their minds. Because it was quite obvious that something was wrong, and this something hung in the air and thickened the atmosphere of the room uncomfortably.

When we had finished supper and Mother and I had cleared the table and taken the dishes out to Jean, we sat down beside the fire as we nearly always did, my chair drawn up near my father's. I became quite sure that the trouble was Mrs. Dorval. I was inexperienced enough and perhaps stupid enough not to realize that any discovery that I had for some months been hiding something from my parents – something of which they could not guess the significance – while going through the usual motions of love, would be a radical shock to them. As we sat there in a waiting silence I felt that there was, between my parents, and between their eyes which looked on one another, a lasting bond woven before my time, and that I, Frankie, had contrived to place myself outside. We had always been three, and there was no constraint amongst us. Tonight we were two, and one. Or so it seemed to me on this evening as I sat there, waiting for something. And I myself had done this, for a stranger, for Mrs. Dorval. Things seemed very confusing. I felt cross with everyone, and I felt a ninny.

FIVE

I sat waiting for someone to begin and arrayed myself for whatever was coming. The dreadful thing was that I was sure that Father and Mother were going to be reasonable and that I would have no chance to feel injured and so take up a strong defensive stand, whatever it was. I had been astonished, a little while before, at what a woman had said to Mrs. Dunne about someone else's father and mother. "Do you know," she said, "that their son told me that he had never in his whole life heard an angry word in his home! His father and mother had never once raised their voices in anger to each other in his whole existence!" I could not see why she was so surprised at this, as I also had never heard an angry word in our home, either in public or private. You could hear every single thing in our house, walls were thin and doors were open, and nothing would have surprised me more and made me more uncomfortable than to hear anger between my father and mother. Of course, they didn't always agree about everything, but that's different. Also, they never spoke angrily to me, although both Mother and Father could be short with me on occasion. But now I sat, fearing the

unknown. Fearing perhaps their anger. The room was
unusually still except for the crackling fire. I looked down at
my fingers.

Mother folded her hands and stretched her arms stiffly
as with effort before her, giving a sigh, and then she relaxed
and said to me, "Frankie, Father and I are very much disturbed,
and we may as well tell you what we have heard, and then you
can tell us what has been happening and why. Last Monday
when Charley Joe came to the kitchen he said to Jean something about Frankie being all the time at Mrs. Dorval's, and
Jean was surprised because she hears everything that goes on
and she'd never heard anything about our knowing this Mrs.
Dorval or you knowing her either, and she said 'Not *our*
Frankie, not Frankie Burnaby, she doesn't know Mrs. Dorval.'
And Charley insisted that he'd seen you there often." (Had he?
When? Oh, the lighted windows!)

Mother paused for a minute and looked at me question-
ingly and Father looked hard at the empty pipe that he was
handling.

I didn't answer at once, because although I had promised
to say nothing about going to see Mrs. Dorval, it came over
me with a rush that the promise was all washed away now that
Mother and Father and probably other people knew. So at last
I said, looking downwards at my twisting fingers, "Yes, I've
been there."

Father spoke in his pleasing growl but his tone was not
pleasing. "How often, Frankie?"

I still looked downwards and said, "Four times, I think,
no, five. Ernestine and I went and looked in at the window
one night."

Then Father exploded. "My daughter a Peeping Tom!"
and I was silent and ashamed.

"Darling," said Mother to Father, "let's hear what Frankie has to say. Frankie, *why* didn't you tell us?" Pause and no answer. "Did you feel there was something wrong about it?" No answer.

"Did this woman tell you *not* to tell?" asked Father, speaking sharply. I disliked Mrs. Dorval being called "this woman," so I looked up and said grandly, "Mrs. Dorval told me she did not want to have callers. She's very fastidious." This was a word I liked, but I did not often have an opportunity to use it. It seemed a splendid word for Mrs. Dorval.

"'*Fastidious*'! My God!" said my father, and jumped up and began to stride up and down the room. I was apprehensive!

"Tell us, Frankie," said Mother patiently, "we still don't really understand why, if there was no harm in it, you should keep it a secret from us. It's either very silly or very wrong. You haven't told us yet. *Did* Mrs. Dorval ask you not to tell that you went to see her?"

I nodded glumly, feeling that a great deal of fuss was being made about nothing much.

Father stopped walking up and down and swung round and stood over me. "What is this lady's reason for not wanting to be called upon. Did she say?"

I tried to remember Mrs. Dorval's words. "Yes, I think she said that she didn't want her life complicated and people running in at all hours. There's nothing wrong in that, is there?" I said miserably.

"And where did you first meet her?" asked Father, still standing over me, tall and brown, extra tall, he seemed.

"Riding into Lytton."

"Frank," interposed Mother, speaking to Father, "I'm sure Frankie promised in all innocence. But darling," (to me) "did you feel comfy about all this? Not telling us, I mean?"

I shook my head and found it hard to keep the tears away.

"The thing that disturbs us is that you should ever have begun to keep anything from Father and me . . ."

"I think, Ellen, I'll have to tell this young lady . . ." interrupted Father, sitting down and polishing his pipe again. And then he told me about Mrs. Dorval. He found it difficult, I could see, to explain to me about "a woman of no reputation." ("Oh," I thought, sitting still and discreet like a bird that is alarmed, "I know, like Nella that went to stay with that rancher, and that woman with the funny hair!" – we children just naturally heard and knew these things) and I learned that Hetty was "a woman of no reputation." Father stopped short there. Apparently he could have said more. In my own mind, seeing Hetty's pure profile and her gentle smile, I said to myself that Father couldn't have believed these things if he had seen her himself. But a sick surprised feeling told me that it might be true.

After a little silence Father said that he would not exact a promise from me that I would not go and see Mrs. Dorval, but he hoped that I saw now why her house was no place for me.

I made one more effort at defence. I looked at each of them imploringly. "Maybe it's all lies that you've heard. She's so sweet and she rides well and she reads books, French books too, and sings lovely songs, and plays the piano, and we don't do things like smoke and drink and play cards for money at her house. Just she sings and we have tea – and she *loved* the wild geese!" I added as a proof of Hetty's innocence.

I suppose the picture of their child carousing with the bad Mrs. Dorval was funny, for Mother smiled across at Father. She got up and put her arm round me. "My funny little daughter!" she said. "Come, let's play Russian Bank."

We spoke no more of Mrs. Dorval but I was greatly troubled. It was just possible, I felt, that Father was wrong. I couldn't think of that strict Mrs. Broom allowing Mrs. Dorval to be wicked even if she wanted to be. And as I thought of Mrs. Dorval looking up at the wild geese and turning to me in rapture, I still could not believe that she was bad.

I came to a decision. Rather dramatically I decided that of course I would "part" from her, but I could not bear that she should think I had deserted her. I would go and say good-bye. Then I would let Father know afterwards. At that thought I quailed, I can tell you!

SIX

I was very much subdued when I left for Lytton on Sunday. I hoped, yet feared, to see Mrs. Dorval on the way. Knowing that I should never feel right with her and with myself if I did not go again to see her and say good-bye, I still dreaded to go. In a sense I had learned to love her very dearly. She was all that I thought beautiful, and so nice to be with. That, I believe, was Hetty's chief equipment for life. She was beautiful, and so nice to be with. I did not meet her on the Lytton road.

I saw Ernestine that Sunday evening. She ran in to Mrs. Dunne's after church to tell me about the circus. The thing was incredible news. Ernestine and I had never seen a circus. "Is it going to be a real circus with lions and elephants and clowns, d'you suppose?" I asked. Ernestine said no, she didn't think so. Not a real circus, just a small travelling fair, and the posters were already in town.

All over the town on Monday a rash of posters broke out. Posters went up and down "the line" and into the hills. They promised a Merry-go-round, and a Ferris Wheel, and a Midway with prizes, and a tattooed man, and a strong man, and a fat lady, and a five-legged calf, and Torquil the Lobster Boy. What was a Lobster Boy?

On Wednesday the youth of Lytton town watched the circus unpacking itself and setting itself up on a large vacant space overlooking the Fraser River. Late on Wednesday the gas flares were burning, the din of the calliope filled the night, the barkers were shouting, the Midway shone with its odd spurious glamour, and the fair was on. Round and round went the lighted Ferris Wheel. Round and round went the lighted Merry-go-round with people clasping the horses. Silent Indians moved slowly out of the darkness into the light and stood watching, or they moved slowly about the little Midway, always watching. The Indians, in small groups, moved always together, as by some inner self-protective compulsion, like certain birds, with their own particular kind of awareness.

Most of the fair people lived in their vans or trailers. Some tried to get lodgings in Lytton. Old Mrs. Anderson who let clean rooms to clean business men was affronted. "Them show people askin' me for rooms!" she said, "No, *sir*! Just let one of 'em in and you'll have the whole lot goin' upstairs usin' the bathroom and God knows what!"

I went to the fair with Ernestine and her father and mother. We walked through the dark quiet Lytton street under a night of stars towards the garish lights and music. The prancing excitement that Ernestine and I felt was all mixed up with the greasy smells from the hot-dog stand; the sudden light and the sudden darkness; the cacophony of sound; motion revolving horizontally, vertically, passing and repassing; drifting town and country people; darting children; barking dogs; all happening together, noise, flare, smell, motion, and the small crowds standing with upturned faces gazing at the picture in front of the lighted booth of Torquil the Lobster Boy.

There hung Torquil's picture on the painted and concealing screen. Torquil was large and pink. He sat upon a sand pile in a marine landscape and looked at nothing. His arms ended in out-size claws or snappers. So did his legs. It was impossible to tell from his picture how Torquil moved about. Was Torquil the subject of some affliction that separated him tragically from his fellows, or did he put on his snappers in the morning, and at night unscrew them and go to bed?

We all crowded in. Torquil sat against a back-drop of whales and fishes. We stared avidly at him as he chewed gum and looked cynically upon us. When he waved his blistered pink flannelly snappers at us a satisfaction filled the crowd. We did not quibble at Torquil for having been boiled until his snappers were red. We drifted on, and on, and circled and swung, and Ernestine and I went to bed that night whirling with lights and music and Torquil the Lobster Boy. I went to sleep to a rhythm – "Torquil the Lobster *Boy*. Torquil the Lobster *Boy*. Torquil the . . ."

Next night we went with some other children and their parents, whom we quickly lost. Suddenly I thought, this is my chance; no one will miss me; and I slipped away from the weaving crowd. Smell and flare melted into noise and noise into flare as I hurried away through the dark street to the other end of Lytton where the houses thinned out to nothing; up the dark slopes with hardly a sound of the calliope in the distance; through the scent of the sage-brush and the noise of the white-laced rushing river, up to where the bungalow showed against the sky. The windows shone square and bright. I went on, without stopping to look in at the window (*"My* daughter a Peeping Tom!"), and knocked on the door. The door opened and showed the solid form of Mrs. Broom with Sailor beside her. She peered at me. "Oh, it's you. Well?"

"Please may I see Mrs. Dorval just a minute?" I asked.

Mrs. Broom did not answer, and I really thought she was going to shut the door in my face when I saw behind her Mrs. Dorval standing. She was in her dressing-gown and I think she must have been ready for bed, for her fair hair was tied back straight from her face and this gave her in the firelight the look of a child.

"Oh," she cried, "it's my faithless Frankie! Where *have* you been? Come in and shut the door."

I did. Mrs. Broom went into the kitchen and Sailor ambled to the hearthrug and lay down.

I stood there gazing at Mrs. Dorval, probably with my face incandescent with the devotion and distress of youth. It flashed through my mind that here I was, all alone, looking at the beautiful Mrs. Dorval, while at the other end of Lytton hundreds of people were paying money to gaze upon Torquil the Lobster Boy. They should have paid money to see Mrs. Dorval. They would have turned and left him.

"Mrs. Dorval," I began, very solemnly I suppose, for she laughed at me and said, "Sit down, Frankie, and don't look so serious. Do you think if you tried hard you could call me Hetty?" And she sat on the couch and leaned forward smiling, her hands clasped upon her knees.

"Oh no, Mrs. Dorval, I couldn't possibly call you Hetty! I wouldn't feel right. And I can't sit down because I've just come to say good-bye."

Hetty's eyebrows grew tragic (which of course meant nothing). "Oh, Frankie, are you going away?"

Here was a way out. "Yes," I said, "I'm going away –" and then with a rush of truthfulness, "but not yet, and that's not why I've come. It isn't that, it's that I mustn't come again. Father and Mother don't know I'm here tonight, but," I gobbled, "I shall tell them because they didn't mean me to come. And I'm sorry, Mrs. Dorval, because I loved it, but I can't come again." There. It was done.

Hetty looked at me and I did not know what she was thinking.

"People are very tiresome," she said thoughtfully. "I have come as far away from people as I can, and yet they go on being tiresome. They make scenes and complicate life terribly. I don't want to have my life complicated and I can't bear scenes. I don't really like women, Frankie – except Mouse, of course – they're the worst, but I thought that you, being just a child . . . and when I saw how you loved the wild geese, I liked you." I nodded.

She looked at the fire a minute and then went on. "I know what they've told you, Frankie. They've told you I'm bad. You must try to believe," she turned her brilliant look on me, "that I'm *not* bad, and that if you knew a little more, you'd understand about it. Can you believe that? . . . Do *you* think I'm bad, Frankie?" she said, laughing a little.

I almost whispered, "No."

"Try and stay my friend," she said. "Even if you can't come to see me, try and stay my friend . . . Very well . . . Good-bye . . ." and with as little emotion as she would have shown in saying good-bye to the postman she got up – she did not come over to touch me – and went into her bedroom and shut the door. It made it easier and harder that she did not come and touch me. She left me standing in the suddenly withdrawn intimacy of the firelit room, with only Sailor sleeping there on the hearth.

I had stood only a moment when Mouse, who must have been listening, came into the room. She opened the front door. "You'd best be going," she said. And I went.

SEVEN

That was on Thursday night. Friday was Empire day and a holiday everywhere. I left for home early on Friday morning and met on the Lillooet road plenty of cars, a waggon or two, an old buggy, a buckboard, Indians on their cayuses with their dogs trotting behind – people going in to Lytton for the fair. I had to pull in to the wayside again and again. When I rode into the yard at the ranch I found Father sitting on the verandah steps. Holidays made not much difference at the ranch, but it was near lunch-time, and so Father was sitting on the steps in the spring sunshine, reading a newspaper three days old, his long legs sprawling out before him. He looked up. "Hello, kid!" he said with a smile, and lowered the newspaper, looking at me with his special kind quick look. I could see that everything was all right now. I jumped off Maxey and ran up and kissed him. I told him all about the fair and sideshows and he listened to me. Then he took up his newspaper again. "Mother's up at the garden," he said and continued his reading. But now I had to tell him about my visit, and get it over. I stood up in front of him in my overalls and buckskin jacket and with my hands behind me.

"Father," I said.

"Well, what?" he said mildly, with his eyes on the page.

"Father, I want to tell you I'm not going to Mrs. Dorval's any more."

"You don't say! Very nice of you, I'm sure," Father said without looking up, in a half-teasing half-sarcastic way he had.

But now was the hard part. I said again, "Father."

"Now, Frankie, it's over and done with, stop harping on it," he said impatiently.

"But, Father, I went there last night again because I had to say good-bye, but I won't go any more."

Father lowered the newspaper and pushed his rancher's broad-brimmed hat back from his forehead and looked at me as if he couldn't believe his eyes and ears.

"Well, I'll be blowed," he said slowly. "I can't understand *you*!"

"But *Father* . . ."

"I don't – want – to – hear – anything – more – about – it," he said pausing emphatically at each word. "You go and talk to your mother." And I left him rattling the newspaper about at arm's length and scowling at the newsprint.

Not long after that last visit of mine to the bungalow Mother told me that they had decided to send me down to the Coast to school, instead of waiting till the following year. Father had begun to think me unpredictable and felt that, as things were, I had too much time on my hands. Yet they did not want to bring me back to the ranch, away from school and all the other children. So at the end of the summer Mother and I drove to the Coast along the great road that hugs the Fraser Canyon, and I went to a little school in Vancouver near

Stanley Park. It was small, with about eight boarders, and we slept in three attic rooms at the top of the tall house. The house was old, there was little equipment of any kind, the fare was plain, but old Mrs. Richards was kind, and Mrs. Brookes, her daughter, was really concerned with education. She brought to the subjects she taught us an interest that was never perfunctory, and our lessons had meaning and direction. I think that old Mrs. Richards was interested in her pupils, while young Mrs. Brookes was interested in their education, and this worked out very well.

We were so near to Stanley Park that it was our playground and paradise. We liked our bedrooms on the top floor because we saw into the Park and across the lagoon. Over the forests of the Park we saw the mountains across the Inlet, and looking the other way, to the west, we could see the waters of English Bay and the great sunsets over the ocean.

There was in our bedroom a large circular mirror of good glass with a cheap old frame. This mirror had been placed, probably by chance, so that it isolated and held a reflection of the Sleeping Beauty. You looked through your window and there the mountains lay loftily to the sky. The Sleeping Beauty's covering of forest, drawn up over her knees, descends into a valley, and from this valley rises another mountain. You turned, and stepped aside, and saw at an angle that the circular mirror had seized and isolated a portion of the beautiful descending and ascending lines of the mountains and the great dark pointed fir trees of the nearby Park below. It became the habit of the four of us in the bedroom to look at our "picture." When our mothers came to see the school we would take them upstairs, and "Look," we would say, "at the picture!" One of us had first discovered it, and on fine days there it was awaiting us in soft clarity. This reflection, held in the circular frame, had more unity and significance than when you turned and saw its substance as only a part of the true, flowing, continuous line of the mountains. I learned from these mountains and from the picture in the mirror the potent and insinuating quality of line, be it in a mountain, or in a tree, or in a human face. And perhaps the others afterwards discovered this and more, far more than I did (because Marcella Martin became an artist). But at that time we gabbled continuously and extravagantly, not about these things but about ourselves and our likes and dislikes, about the "thrilling" or the "loathsome" hockey, the heavenly swimming, the school play, the bread puddings, our friends and their brothers, a new dress and "what Marion said. My dear, it was a scream!" – these were the things which mattered so much then, and which are now almost forgotten, while what remains clearer and more lasting even than the cheerful reality of old Mrs. Richards beaming anxiously behind a large brown teapot, is a still reflection of mountains in a round mirror.

It was at the end of my last term at Mrs. Richards' that I saw Hetty Dorval again.

Three of us were in the town, choosing a good-bye present for old Mrs. Richards. As we leaned over the counter, I looked up, and there, across the large jewellery store, was Hetty. She was as beautiful there as when, in Lytton, no one had challenged comparison, and she made everyone else in the shop appear ordinary. She held up a string of pearls and looked at them, intent, her pretty head tilted connoisseur-wise. Mrs. Broom stood beside her. Hetty turned to Mrs. Broom and spoke. I could almost hear her tone, cajoling, "Mouse, *which* would you have if you were me?" I looked away from her in something like panic. I did not want, now, to be enthralled by or involved with Hetty again. Neither, did

I imagine, would Hetty welcome a school girl in a navy blue uniform. Mouse certainly would not. So I turned my back on where they stood, and bent over the counter once more. I felt a little shamefaced and agitated.

Mother had been very clever about Hetty. Mother was no psychologist by the book, but she had a good working knowledge of human beings. Instead of keeping the Hetty episode as a dark corner of my young life, Hetty was trotted out into the open, but only when it seemed natural. "You mustn't mind, Frankie, but Father and I always call her The Menace, because she was, you know." Mother had never seen Hetty, and I could not bring myself to try, and to fail, to describe what Hetty looked like, and the feeling that she gave people. I should have sounded silly.

The importance and excitement of my last week at school vanished and never returned, with the news that Ernestine had been drowned in trying to save her dog. When we are young we have, by nature, no concern with permanent change or with death. Life is forever. Then suddenly comes the moment when death makes the entrance into experience, very simply, inexorably; our awareness is enlarged and we move forward with dismay into the common lot, and the bright innocent sureness of permanency has left us. There had never been a time when I could not remember my almost daily companion Ernestine; she was my very particular friend and I was hers, and nearly all our fun (and that was nearly all our life) had been together. And now Ernestine, not I, had waded regardless into the dull swirling shallows of the Fraser River and got caught in the current, and was gone. I was aghast at the mysterious ceasing-to-be of Ernestine, and in a new awe of her. On the journey home I had always watched with happy rising excitement for the first small bunch of sage growing beside the railroad track ("There it is!") which signified the change in vegetation, the beginning of the sage-brush country, Lytton, and home. But now I was only gloomily aware of it and of the slowing up of the train at Lytton station, which looked surprisingly the same as before. But Mother and Father were waiting there. I saw Mother's raised face and her bright eyes searching the windows with the comfort of a familiar and loving look. – Do you not know it, that look? – We drove away across the Bridge and along the dusty hairpin road, home.

Perhaps it was the death of Ernestine that hastened Father's and Mother's plans. I don't know. But I found that Mother and I were really going to England in the late autumn. We began our serious preparations and I my excited good-byes. Mother alternated between joy at going and a resolve not to leave Father. She would go. My spirits rose. She would not go. My spirits sank. Father said she was going, and no non-sense. Again she would go.

Three days before we left, Father drove down to the rancheree where Joe Charley lived, to get some Indians to help at the ranch before the good weather broke completely, and Mother and I went with him. We always drove with Father, that last week, wherever he went. Three sit crowded in the front seat, talking and laughing together. Because this is, perhaps, the last drive, each is in his own degree projected into the future, which at that moment joins the flying present and the past. No one says so, but each one is aware within – we shall be gone, he will be here – they will be gone, I shall be here. Those who make a real and long departure of years, see the familiar road, houses, trees, shops, people, the sage-brush and the hills, the cat, the dog – and a difference lies upon these objects. Each common thing bears the strange mark of something which we are imminently leaving behind, which we shall not hereafter customarily see as before, but which is intrinsically real and will remain in its own place. And so it was then as we drove about Lytton and the surrounding country with Father.

After crossing the Bridge and the rivers that day we drove east, and as we neared the fork that led downhill to the rancheree beside the river, Mother said to Father, "Frank, I've never seen the place where The Menace used to live. Turn up to the right, it's only a little way!" And Father turned to the right and stopped at the top of the slope as we saw the bungalow, and Mother and I got out and went round to each window. The wind blew fresh up there. The sage-brush spread for miles before your eyes, and sage had invaded the garden.

"She left here over a year ago, you know, Frankie. No one seemed to know why," said Mother. "I don't know where she is, menacing about, now, but someone from Lytton saw her in Vancouver not long ago. And quite affluent." And I said that I had seen her too, just that once, looking at the pearls. Ernestine, and leaving school, and coming home, had quite put Hetty out of my mind.

Mother and I could not get into the bungalow any where, but we turned and stood on the broad porch, looking down on the rapids of the river bright and noisy below, and across at the great back-drop of dun-coloured hills desolate under a blue sky. Father honked the horn. "Come here, Frank," called Mother. "Do come. Just for a minute. I want to show you."

Father, doing his pretend grumbling, got out and came over to us. Two things about Father. He was a man of some substance and a good rancher, and he could wear a hat better than anyone I ever saw. It didn't matter whether it was his old wide-brimmed ranch hat or his town hat. On went the hat –

smack – with Father's genius for angle. He came over to the porch and stood with us there and looked north, east, and west.

"Good old Menace," he said, "she certainly picked a view!" (Good old Menace! – but then Father hadn't seen Hetty.) And we all stood looking.

When we reached the dilapidated long shack where Joe Charley lived, Mother and I waited outside while Father went to find someone to speak to. The rancheree looked forsaken. Most of the Indians had gone to town. One or two dogs came and barked at us, a few hens scratched in the dust, some children peeped shyly, and then a squaw followed by two young girls came out of a house like Joe Charley's. Father gave them the message and we drove away.

When we got near Lytton, Mother said, "Frank, you'll say I'm crazy. All right, I'm crazy. But I want to get the key for that bungalow and really go inside. You get it from the real estate office and Frankie and I will go to Wong's and get him to make up a picnic lunch and we'll go back and have a picnic there. Do let's."

So Mother and I went to the Chinese café and got a picnic lunch and a thermos from Wong, and Father went to Bellamy's for the key. We drove up the hill again and got out. Father unlocked the door and we all went in.

Mrs. Broom had made a neat business of leaving the house, just as she had of going into it. There was none of the litter and exhaustion of an empty and deserted dwelling. Just a neat little, square little, scrubbed little bungalow, with a fireplace, and book-shelves made specially for Hetty Dorval, and two bedrooms, a bathroom of sorts, and a kitchen; and in front, a broad porch overlooking the river. I did not work up any sentiment about the room that could look and had looked so warm and confiding. It seemed better to me as it was that sunny day with Mother and Father, more comfortable, although it is true that without the presence of Hetty and all that surrounded her the place felt emptier than empty. To begin with, I think that Mother had wanted to exorcise the bungalow completely, superimposing on my youthful memory which she and Father could not share, the picture of us three together there, dispelling the memory of her little daughter and the stranger. Then she fell in love with the bungalow, and Father played right into her hands.

"Bellamy tells me," he said, shoving his hat back, "that the place could be bought for a song. They want to wind up the old Absalom estate and they'd almost give it away."

Mother whirled round and her eyes sparkled. "Then give it to me, Frank! I want it! I adore it! Let's have it!"

"Whatever for? Don't you like the ranch? Your mother doesn't like her old home, Frankie!"

"Darling, don't be *so* silly! You know I love the ranch. But when you and I are old, old people and we don't want to work any more, wouldn't it be lovely to have this little bungalow on the hill-side!"

"Listen to your mother!" said Father smiling "Thinks I'm made of money."

"And then we could rent it and make some money in the meantime," said Mother in jerks, pulling and pushing at a window.

The bungalow was a true log house, and the windows slid in grooves, to open. But the windows had grown into their places, so we pushed and pulled until we had them all open and the wind blew freely through.

"*There!*" said Mother, waving her hands to the wind as if to say "Come on," and I knew exactly what she was doing. She was blowing Hetty Dorval right out of the house.

We sat down on the porch and ate Wong's lunch and Mother said, "The thing about this place, Frank, is that you don't have to buy the hills opposite. They're all yours. No one's ever going to use them – look, there's the train!"

The melancholy hoot of the train creeping along beside the river below on its long journey across a continent was the only sign of the outside world, and comfortably remote. Here life would be very simple. Nothing and no one could complicate life here, Mother was saying. Couldn't they? ("I will *not* complicate my life!")

When we finished lunch we fell silent, and Father lay down on the flat boards and went to sleep. He could sleep anywhere. On a long rough run he could stretch his length on the running board of his car and sleep, and then drive on refreshed. He was famous for it.

We drove rather silently back to Lytton. We took the thermos back to Wong who stood outside his café in the bright sunshine. His grandchildren played near the door. Wong was an old fat Chinaman whose father was one of the Chinese who mined for gold in the Fraser and in the Cariboo country in the early sixties. Wong was born up country and he still spoke perversely among the risen generation the kind of English that his father spoke.

"What for you go away, Frankie?" he asked me. "You heap crazy. You smart girl, you stay home. Bimeby large trouble. *Sure,*" nodding sagaciously. "I read my China paper tell me. Large trouble Jap-ann. Large trouble Lush" (that was Russia). "Large trouble Yulip" (Yulip to rhyme with Tulip was Europe). "You stay home, I know! I tell you the truth, Frankie!" But I was nearly sixteen and I did not care about trouble in Yulip.

I realize now, as I write, that Wong was a rarely happy man. Philosophical, kind, cynical, amused, shrewd, comfortable, and as powerful as he cared to be. He served many, but was a servant to no one. He said good-bye to us, turned and went into his shop, still nodding, omniscient.

Late that afternoon I said the last of my farewells, to my old friend and teacher at the Convent-Hospital, Sister Marie-Cécile. She stood, a sturdy black and white figure, waving till we had driven out of sight.

The sun had dipped behind the hills and a wind had risen and was blowing cold against us down the channel of the Fraser as we drove home on the Lillooet road. There was so much to think of and so much to do that Mother forgot all about the bungalow; at least, she spoke no more of it to Father, as far as I knew. But next Christmas Day, at old Mr. Trethewey's house in Cornwall, Mother received a cable which read, "Happy Christmas to both my girls stop hope you will like your bungalow Ellen all my love."

So now Hetty Dorval's bungalow belonged to my mother, and my mother had opened the windows and Hetty had been blown out and away. The bungalow had almost begun to mean to me not Hetty, but "That picnic we had on nearly the last day – you remember?" and Father lying there, asleep in the sunshine.

EIGHT

To be on the ocean, out of sight of land, on an actual sea voyage, and to be sixteen, was then very pleasant. One regards it now as through the wrong end of a telescope. It is illogically remote and disproportionate. On the first day of this voyage, when you are not yet initiated, you watch with respect the passengers being born into this new world which will shortly detach itself from the land world and move off into oceanic space. Passengers are born into this new world via the gang-plank and are delivered by accoucheurs, stewards and others, to whom this is no phenomenon. These passengers, male and female, wear their best hats and usually their best clothes. The reason for this is that their best clothes take more trouble to pack than their old clothes. Moreover, they are more impressive when the passengers board the liner. The next day, or soon afterwards, you identify some of these passengers, not by their clothes which are different and certainly not by their hats which are as different as possible, but by such slight landmarks as noses and chins, or sometimes by the recognition of a striking and memorable face. All this is

familiar to veteran travellers, but not to you. Some of these
passengers then become torpid in deck chairs. But you are not
torpid, because you are sixteen. You have joined a small mobile
aristocracy whose members at first eyed each other specula-
tively and even with suspicion, but have since quickly become
a closed corporation to which admission is the fact of being
sixteen or seventeen but you must have some other commend-
able quality as well. There are usually hangers-on to this aristocracy who are persons of fifteen or less, but they hardly
count. Also, you have become mildly in love with a young
American girl (if you are a boy), or with a young American
boy (if you are a girl), and you forget that the journey will ever
come to an end. You are not sea-sick. Oh no. The lurch and
plunge of the ship, the walloping slap of the ocean upon its
side, and the buffeting winds are part of your delusion and
your enjoyment. People who succumb to sea-sickness, usually
adults, are negligible to you and worthy of being despised, for
you have not yet learned compassion the hard way. The dining
saloon is the seventh heaven, and you who have all your life
helped with the dinner dishes at home, now gorge yourself in
a superior and affluent manner (it costs no more) with the
skilled aid of stewards and music. That the journey will end,
you do not consider until suddenly it has ended. Life was still
like that when Mother and I went away.

As Mother and I, still fellow travellers, leaned on the
ship's rail watching the other passengers coming aboard and
standing about in small talking groups amongst all the exciting weaving sounds of meeting, parting and departing, Mother
touched my arm. "Frankie," she said, "don't look now, but
there's a woman with a most heavenly profile. Angelic! She's
standing talking to a little old man and one of the ship's

officers. At least *she's* not talking, they're talking to her, and as pleased with themselves as two peacocks. Oh, don't turn now, she's looking our way."

I turned as soon as I thought it safe, and I feel now that before I turned I felt a pricking in my thumbs. Perhaps not. Well, I turned, and by this time the woman had stopped looking in our direction and was again listening to the two men in a way infinitely gentle and pretty. It was Hetty. I gave a little gasp. "What, Frankie?" asked Mother.

"Mother," I said very quietly, "you won't believe me, but that's Mrs. Dorval."

Mother turned and faced me, all seriousness. "Frankie! You don't mean that!" She paused. "So *that* is The Menace! Frankie, I can't believe it. Not *that* girl! She can't be Mrs. Dorval!"

"She is, Mother. That's exactly who she is and that's what she looks like. Do you see now why I couldn't explain?" I said. "What am I going to do about it?"

"I don't *think*," said Mother slowly, "that Mrs. Dorval will come our way. She won't be interested in two women travelling together, at least a woman and a girl, and it doesn't matter whether she is or not. But we'll keep our own counsel, Frankie. Well, I'm amazed! What a peculiar thing . . ." and Mother went on murmuring diminuendo.

I was rather shaken when we went down to our cabin. Fate was indeed throwing Hetty at us. But perhaps Hetty would not be thrown. We would see. She would do whatever suited her best.

We passed near each other once or twice during the day, but Hetty gave no sign. One would say that she did not see me. Of course, she might not at once know me, but a look at the passenger list, and the word "Lytton," would recall my name and home. I saw Mrs. Broom, walking alone. But Mrs. Broom was a woman whom one could easily not notice, in contrast to Hetty; and Mrs. Broom was herself an expert at not noticing anyone.

Really to know the ocean, really to know that you are at sea, you must, in the dark, go out and feel the invisible wind and look out into the illimitable night. And perhaps if you look down over the rail you will see bright phosphorus tearing at the ship's sides. Mother and I went out when it was dark to watch, too, the dwindling twinkling lights of land, each of which has a human significance in that place which it illumines. We could now hardly see the outline of the dark and faintly spangled shore. Many other passengers, leaning in twos and threes, also gazed into the dark. Before long I felt someone move up beside me. This was not accident, this was design. This person knew me, and had moved near to me because she knew me. I felt this, and was aware that she was about to speak. I could not see the face clearly but I knew that the person was Hetty.

"Frankie," the very soft voice said hurriedly in the dark, "and your Mother? Mrs. . . . Burnaby? Just one word. Please. I must speak to you tonight. Frankie, you were my friend once . . . for a little while. I don't know whether you are now or not. And you, Mrs. Burnaby, I cannot tell . . . but I think you are kind, and I'm casting myself on your generosity, both of you." Hetty's voice, usually indifferent and light, was urgent. I heard fear there. "I am going to be married, soon. I am marrying General Connot as soon as we land. He's old, Mrs. Burnaby, but he knows about me. He knew me before, when I was nearly as young as Frankie." (Was this woman of unknown experience really ever a girl like me?) "I shan't trouble you at all, I promise, but please . . . it's hard for me to ask this . . .

can you forget that you ever knew me or heard my name? I want security," her voice trembled a little, "I want it badly, and you can take it from me if you talk about me. Do you understand, Frankie? . . . *You* understand, Mrs. Burnaby, don't you? I had to speak now, I couldn't wait."

All the time that Hetty was speaking hurriedly and softly people were passing and re-passing in their evening promenade. A small man walked slowly with little steps along the line of leaning passengers, scrutinizing each dark figure and group beside the rail. He stopped near us and Hetty was as though she had not spoken. He recognized her whom he sought and said with relief in his voice, "Hetty, my dear! I lost you, where have you been?" and they moved away together.

It was hard to tell how much of Hetty was artful and how much was artless. But we knew that when she spoke to us she was sincere and frightened, and that we held her in our hands, and I think that whatever Hetty in her time had done to other women, Mother felt sorry for her. Mother was unsentimental, I would say, but she was quick to see and quick to sympathize. Women, and board-ship, and gossip – and Hetty must have known that she was too conspicuous to escape. We could easily do her irrevocable harm.

In our cabin Mother said, "You know, Frankie, I'm always inclined to mistrust a tremble in a woman's voice. They do it on purpose, some of them. I've heard them and I always want to tremble back for fun when it's just dramatizing. But if it's real, then you pay attention, Frankie, because that's when someone needs help or – anyway – understanding. And this was real. That woman is frightened of losing this security, and she very nearly has it. Perhaps she didn't want it once, but she wants it now. Don't let's speak any more about her, Frankie, in case we make a slip of some kind and hurt her. It would be awfully easy. There's no need to do that. She is none of our affair now. She says this man knows about her. So let you and me be the three monkeys." And we were.

I soon joined the confederacy of the young. We were not many but as far as we were concerned the ship was ours, with a reservation of deference to the ship's officers. We were not intentionally rude to the grown-ups who lay and walked about the place. For the most part we did not see them; we only saw each other; simply they were not there. We were engrossed in our concerns. We played all day; we danced all evening; the rest of the time we ate and slept. Yet in the day-time and in the evening too I was aware of Hetty. It felt queer to be so near to her, without recognition. Even the board-ship critics, it seemed, could find small cause for gossip about her, although everyone noticed her. That was inevitable. Her only faults were that she engaged the attention of too many men without seeming to try to do so, and that she did not respond to nor placate the women. She was adept at being sweetly vague and un-noticing. Her very activities were passive, not active – if you can call it an activity to sit still and appear unconsciously lovely – and so she could not be blamed if the men liked to sit near her and talk, or if sometimes they asked her to sing. Billy Stocker and I, stopping near the Palm Room doors after dinner, sometimes heard the sound of a sweet true voice, singing. Hetty was sitting at the piano and singing as she sang to me at Lytton, partly because Sir Terence Connot asked her to and partly because she loved singing. Three or four men sat near in retrospective attitudes and old General Connot watched her. "I could if I would," I thought as I looked at Hetty. But Mother and I were true to our ungiven word and Hetty landed safely in England.

A letter written in a large and simple hand reached me a few weeks later. It came from Bath and had been sent to me at Lytton to be forwarded. It read:

"Dear Frankie,
  "Thank you –
    "Hetty Connot."

So now Hetty was Lady Connot. Mother and I felt that we were never likely to see her again but that still we should say nothing because you never can tell. For, as we told each other, we might, by way of being entertaining, relate the story of Hetty Dorval as it had concerned us, with all its damaging inferences, to someone who might turn out to be General Connot's sister-in-law, or niece, or friend, unawares, and thereby cause more trouble than we should care for or could undo.

Mother had at last admitted to me that a very ugly story had followed Hetty from Shanghai to Vancouver and so to Lytton. But she did not know the actual truth of it.

NINE

The genius loci is an incalculable godling whose presence is felt by many people but certainly not by all. Many experience his presence but who knows his name and all his attributes? I have heard that some people who live on our Canadian prairie and are therefore used to flat spaces and far horizons, cannot for long endure even the medium-sized mountains of the Pacific coast. Others from the same prairie, however, find on our mountainous shore their true home. There is no rule about it. The thing goes deeper than like and dislike. It is the genius. To some the genius of a place is inimical; to some it is kind. Marcella Martin, who was a boarder with me at Mrs. Richards' school, and older than I am, told me that she once went for a holiday with her parents to a valley in the high mountains of Oregon. The mountains ringed them closely round, Marcella said, rising abruptly from the near edge of their camping ground, treading on their toes by day and falling on their heads by night. Everyone but Marcella seemed to think this delightful. Marcella did not dare to confide to her parents that the claustrophobic effect of the mountains was driving her mad. She became depressed and nervous, and when she heard that, the week before, a very nice young woman had been taken away "raving mad," she knew perfectly well that the reason was not an unhappy love affair as was said, but that the immoderate mountains had done it. And she became very frightened. When she returned to Vancouver where the mountains are beautiful but moderate and are at a moderate distance, she became herself again and never had a recurrence of this disturbance. Of course, Marcella was an artist whose sensibility may have made her an easy prey to the rapacious god in that place.

My genius of place is a god of water. I have lived where two rivers flow together, and beside the brattling noise of China Creek which tumbles past our ranch house and turns our water wheel, and on the shore of the Pacific Ocean too – my home is there, and I shall go back. And so, when we came to England I was glad that we were to be beside the ocean. Mother's godfather, old Mr. Trethewey, lived on the Cornish coast, and it was to his house set on the cliffs high above the windy Atlantic that we had a warm welcome.

When we landed, and all the fun of the days on board ship was behind us, I felt that nothing could ever be as good again. The thrills had gone to my head and I was a little above myself. In the train on the way to Cornwall I was moody and homesick for the ship's friendships which had grown with tropical speed and were all scattered now. The future was bleak or perhaps mouldy – an old gentleman, a grown-up man, a very young girl, and an unknown boarding-school. Mother looked out of the window, reviving memories of green England. I looked too, and half the time I did not see England at all. It would have been pleasant enough if my mind had not been busy re-living the electric days just over. I looked at the future.

"Mother," I said in a lofty tone that I had just acquired, "how old is this Molly Trethewey?"

"Molly? Oh, about twelve or thirteen – perhaps fourteen – I don't know," said Mother.

"Oh, just a kid!" I said, in my new loftiest manner. This did not have a good effect on Mother.

"Frankie, you can be very irritating," she said coolly. "You have been getting a bit too bumptious the last few days. It's a good thing for you that the ocean voyage ended, it was about a day too long. I'd like to remind you that *you* were fourteen two years ago, and that up till now the world owes you nothing whatever. You owe the world everything and now you are being offered a home by Uncle David Trethewey and his nephew Richard and his niece Molly and it doesn't matter what age she is. She can be two if she likes. And moreover," looking at her wrist watch, "you've got just about an hour in which to get natural again, and not be a silly ass like that Pamela Something on the ship." And Mother turned to the window and continued to look out with detached interest.

Well really! Me! Irritating! Bumptious! Well! Mother must have been saving this up for a day or two, the way she said it.

I should like to describe Molly and Richard and their guardian, "our" Uncle David Trethewey, because they are very important to me and have meant a great deal in my life, and now they always will. But this is not a story of me, nor of them, in a way, but of the places and ways known to me in which Hetty Dorval has appeared. It is not even Hetty Dorval's whole story because to this day I do not know Hetty's whole story and she does not tell. I only knew the story of Hetty by inference and by strange chance. Circumstances sometimes make it possible to know people with sureness and therefore with joy or some other emotion, because continuous association with them makes them as known and predictable as the familiar beloved contours of home, or else the place where one merely waits for the street car, or else the dentist's drill. Take your choice. But one cannot invade and discover the closed or hidden places of a person like Hetty Dorval with whom one's associations, though significant, are fragmentary, and for the added reason that Hetty does not speak – of herself. And therefore her gently impervious and deliberately concealing exterior does not permit her to be known. One guesses only from what one discerns. Any positive efforts that one could discern on the part of Hetty were directed towards isolating herself from responsibilities to other people. She endeavoured to island herself in her own particular world of comfort and irresponsibility. ("I will *not* have my life complicated.") But "No man is an Iland, intire of it selfe"; said Mother's poet three hundred years ago, and Hetty could not island herself, because we impinge on each other, we touch, we glance, we press, we touch again, we cannot escape. "No man is an Iland." Who touched me? . . .

And so I will write down something about Richard and Molly who were candid and knowable, and whom I came to love so well. I must write it because their relationship to each other, and to myself, is part of the story of Hetty Dorval.

Richard and Molly are brother and sister born with years between them of parents who died when Molly was five years old and Richard a boy of eighteen.

Richard at once took Molly as his care. He was not only a brother, he was all the father and mother and nurse that a big boy can be to a little sister. Although their father's older brother – our Uncle David – became their real guardian and Molly lived in his home, Richard felt all a big brother's solicitude for her, and shared her guardianship with her uncle, who encouraged this. Molly on her side lived her happy child's life by the sea with her uncle, looking always for Richard's returnings from Cambridge, and later from the journeys near and far on which he was sent by his engineering firm.

During the short week that Mother and I first spent at Cliff House we soon understood this. Richard was there in essence, for he seemed to be the complement of Molly's life and of Uncle David's too, and the near coming of Christmas meant the coming of Richard. During that week, this little nut-brown Molly taught me the neighbourhood. We went together down the hill to the village and the quay and watched the fishermen at their boats and at their nets. While Mother and Uncle David talked their long renewing talks, Molly and I climbed amongst the heather. Nothing lay between the house and the edge of the cliff but heather. There seemed to be a very large quantity of sky above for so small a country as England, I thought, and at the foot of the cliffs, from tide marks to horizon, lay the ocean. There was smallness, but there were horizons, too. I discovered that English skies are large, and whether they are dull and lowering, or luminously moist and grey, or blue with infinitely great and billowing white clouds, they have a particular quality of space and Englishness. When Mother and I left to do the school-hunting business that had to be finished before Christmas week, Uncle David and Molly were established in my affection as people I belonged with and wanted to come back to.

Father's cable about the bungalow came to Mother on Christmas Day, and Mother was half laughing and half crying. I realized that the bond between Mother and Father was so close that this separation of six thousand miles was like a physical hurt to Mother, and Christmas made it worse.

Uncle David, Richard and Molly were kind and perfect, but that was not enough. I would have been entirely happy in this English Christmas had it not been for the queer infusion of distress for Mother and the realization that, love her as I did and as she loved me, we were all of us as shadows to her compared with Father. When Mother's loving duty was done to me and I was cheerfully settled at school near London, she left England for home with unrestrained delight.

Cliff House to me means being on the heather on the high cliffs looking out to sea, with a big wind blowing in from the West and the ocean booming in the caves below. It means Molly with her brown hair streaming back, facing the sky, the wind, the wheeling gulls, the sound of the everlasting breakers and the sparkling sea beyond – all bright sight, sound, scent and the coarse feel of the heather mingled together with us in one bright moment – and saying, "Oh Richard, if we could keep minutes like this for always!" and Richard saying lazily, "You can, if you realize it hard enough now." And Molly teasing Richard – "Rick, why don't you marry Frankie and we'll all live here happy ever after?" and Richard saying, "Perhaps I will if she'll have me when she's old enough," and Molly, "Old enough! She'll soon be eighteen!"

Sometimes Richard brought friends with him to Cliff House. Uncle David rented a pony for me (it was wonderful to feel something like Maxey under me again, but the saddle was different) and we rode together, Uncle David and all of us. We bicycled, bathed, rowed, fished, sailed, and came home hungry to large teas of fresh Cornish splits piled with strawberry jam and Cornish cream, and in the winter-time to a fire on the hearth. This happened so often – Easter, summer and Christmas too – that it came to seem like a happy perpetuity. And more than two years passed by.

Gradually Richard began to look upon me as an individual and almost a grown-up, not just as Molly's friend, young Frankie Burnaby from Canada. He began to talk to me about Molly's education. What shall we do next? What change of school? When? And what then? What did she need? What did I think? – Uncle David would agree. This pleased me, not only because it showed that Richard liked me and felt confidence in me, but because I had come to think of Molly almost as mine, and I was beginning to assume a big sister's responsibility for her. I did not think of Richard yet as a brother or as a friend or as a lover. He was just Richard.

As I look back, I don't know when or where my liking for Richard began or ended. I accepted my liking or perhaps my love for him without question. It was all natural and completely young and happy. Nothing spoiled the harmony and confidence of our lives together, whether we were apart, or whether we were all together in Cliff House, by the sea. I had not thought of Hetty for a very long time.

TEN

I now received a heavy blow. One day in December Richard came to the school to see me and brought the news of Father's death. Father's truck had gone off the icy road of the Fraser Canyon. He had been taken to the Convent-Hospital, and there they had brought Mother to him. I wanted to go at once to Mother. But telegrams and a letter from her and a long letter from Sister Marie-Cécile reiterated that Mother was well, that she knew what she had to do, and that I was on no account to change the plans that they had made for me. She might even join me in a little while but of that she could not speak with any certainty – not yet.

Sister Marie-Cécile wrote (and I will set part of it down in English): "Your mother told me to tell you everything, my dear Frances, and I will tell you, for there are things which she could not write to you although you should know them. I will tell you, Frances, for I was with her, that just before your father ceased to live he said to her 'Dear, our happy, happy life together,' and your mother said without weeping, 'Nothing can ever part you and me, Frank. We shall always be together wherever we are, my dear love.' And then I heard the word

'Frankie.' Your mother could not tell you these things but you are grown-up now and they are yours to keep. Your mother did not break down, she is very strong and she is good, and I want you to be aware, Frances, that your parents have between them the perfection of human love. They are not of our Faith, but they still have the gift of God. Do as your mother bids you, dear child, and you will make things easier for her. Mr. Baker says that he will run the ranch together with his, with the hired help that your father has had, and some arrangement can be come to later and your mother will go to her friends in Victoria for a while. There she will make up her mind what to do about the ranch, and she may, she says, come then and join you. But things in Europe seem very unsettled, perhaps we shall all know more soon. Your mother is writing to you."

The letter finished. As I read I saw my mother leaning over my father in the immortal attitude of love. I do not know whether I grieved most for my tall strong slow-moving father who had gone in one false moment of Time, or for my mother whose life-spring was in him. Those two were as much part of me in their unitedness and their beauty and their inevitability as were day and night.

And so it was that after Christmas I went up to London as had been already planned, and prepared to go to Paris for six months with Paula Fairfax, who had just left the school too. Paula had stayed once before with a French family called Lafontaine, and Mme. Lafontaine had room in her house for us both. Before the news came of Father's death, Paula and I had been excited and happy. She knew Paris, we both knew French, we were friends, we felt emancipated and important. The plan had been that next we should both return to London and share a room together while we each took a secretarial course. Then I was to say good-bye to Uncle David and Rick and Molly, and go back to Mother and Father, having accomplished at least part of what I had been sent to England to do. And now this was changed. And yet not changed, for Mother insisted that I should do as Father and she had planned. So in January I went up to London and joined Paula. If Richard was to be in town, Molly would come up in a few days, and Molly, Rick and I would have a farewell celebration. We had never felt so close together, we of Cliff House, as now, when I was to leave them.

There was great uneasiness everywhere in the public and private mind, and the word "War" underlay everybody's thoughts.

ELEVEN

On Wednesday Paula and I were to leave for Paris. On Monday Molly came up to London and we shopped and had tea and Rick took us to a play at the Haymarket. The next day we were to meet Richard at Scott's in Piccadilly for lunch, and to say good-bye. Then I was to join Paula, and Rick would take Molly to see friends of Uncle David's in the afternoon. The next day we were all going away, Rick to his firm's Branch in Edinburgh, Molly back to Cliff House, and I to Paris.

In spite of the ever-present trouble of Father's death I was more happy than I would ever have thought possible, and this was what Uncle David, Rick and Molly had hoped the diversion would do for me. Molly and I waited outside Scott's and then we saw Rick coming through the crowd. Molly was pretty and brown. Her chunky schoolgirl figure was lengthening out into slenderness but her laughing face was still the face of a child. Rick took hold of us and piloted us both into Scott's and we were taken to a room upstairs. We followed the waiter across the room to a table near the window. Beside the window, at a smaller table, waiting to be served, sat a woman in mourning, or at least in black. She was not looking in our direction. Her graceful head was turned towards the window. The line of her profile was pure and a little sad. The curve of her softly rounded and rather high cheek-bone and the soft hollow beneath, the tilted "flirt's nose," and the rather over-full upper lip – all gave me a faint shock of delight and then of sudden alarm. It was Hetty, in a black hat of simplicity and great smartness, looking down through the window at the crowds in Piccadilly, but looking down in her own special way, not like any other woman who looks out of a window. I felt Rick's eyes rest upon her, I felt Molly look at her too, and I thought "Now I'm for it, let's run!" – when Hetty slowly turned her head and looked up at me, and for a full moment gave us her long, careless, gentle look. I stood there, a girl of nearly nineteen – no, a child of twelve. (Mother, you dear little dragon, why aren't you here!) Something was held suspended. The waiter moved a chair. Hetty's eyebrows raised in tragic pleasure and recognition and her face was lit by her brilliant look. "Frankie!" she said in a soft tone of delight. She held up her hand, palm upwards, and there was all giving, all welcome in the gesture.

And then she said, "Is your mother in England?" And in answer to my dissenting head, "No?" But the question seemed to establish her as a family friend.

And then she said softly, but clearly enough for Rick and Molly to hear, "You know, Frankie, that Terence died?" How should I know? Why, indeed, should I care? But one thing I knew, that Richard and Molly were thinking "What a marvellous creature! Why did Frankie never tell us! Her husband has died! Frankie and she are old friends! How sad she is! Let us all sit together."

And then Hetty turned her softened serene gaze on Rick and Molly, and in the almost imperceptible movement of the hand there was deprecation and apology and inclusion. The thing was done.

So interested were Rick and Molly in my beautiful friend that I think they did not notice my gaucherie as I stood there. I soon observed that Hetty had ascertained at once that Mother was not there, and Mother's absence, if Hetty should have plans, made things easier for her, of course. From the very moment that I saw that pure profile I knew I was in for trouble. But I could not stand there indefinitely. There was only one thing to do and I could not pass by. Hetty's gentle gesture had already included Rick and Molly, not boldly of course, but definitely. Waiters could not stand still forever. Life in Scott's Restaurant could not be arrested while Frankie Burnaby cast about in her mind how on earth to cope with Hetty Dorval. So I said rather primly (I thought), "Lady Connot, this is Molly Trethewey and Mr. Richard Trethewey." Very stiff, I thought. But already the waiter was conveying with all his insinuating skill but without uttering a word that our table was for four, and if my great friend Lady Connot would join us there would be one more table free, and please to make up our minds though of course it didn't matter to him if he stood there and smiled all day, oh, not at all. And while all this was materializing in the air Richard said, in the kindness of his heart to me, but most particularly I think because my great friend Lady Connot was so pathetic and so utterly beautiful, and because Terence (whoever that was) had died, and because Molly was all dancing eyes and anticipation and would enjoy the party, and because our tables were side by side and it would have been silly not to – because of all these things,

Richard turned to me and said with his charming smile, "Won't Lady Connot join us?" Lady Connot would, and moving to our table in her simple black elegance, Lady Connot did. "What a delightful party!" everybody seemed to say.

And Lady Connot was telling them, before ever we perused the yards of menu which the waiter gave us, that the first time she ever saw ("ever" had the implication of old friendship and many meetings), the first time she ever saw Frankie, Frankie was loping, western style, along the foot of a sage-brush hill, wearing an Indian buckskin jacket. "And do you remember the wild geese going over-head, Frankie?" said Hetty, turning her beauty on me. Yes, I remembered the wild geese all right, and I wished I was looking at them then, and was not in Scott's Restaurant, Piccadilly, with the two people I loved next to best in the world, perhaps best in the world in a way at that moment, and watching them succumbing to the flowing slow-spoken charm of Hetty Dorval and me not able to do a thing about it. And *did* I remember Sailor the dog? And then we were away on dogs. Dogs. Dogs. Dogs. By this time we were all one.

I prodded myself, contrariwise, for being suspicious and unfair to Hetty. But my main preoccupation was how should I manage about that ensnaring business of Hetty's. I had felt very adult ten minutes before, being a young woman in her nicest clothes who had left school and was just going to Paris, lunching at Scott's in some style with a very prepossessing man and a suitably dressed and pretty young girl. Ten minutes before I had been almost a woman of the world. The encounter with Hetty had put me back in the Lytton school-room. "I'll bet," I thought, "dollars to doughnuts, Hetty was looking out of the window and saw us coming. Then the play with the profile, then the look, and 'Frankie!' with that

delighted welcome; and then, 'Is your mother in England?';
then (very softly) 'Did you know that Terence had died?'" The
pattern fell into its place. How much of Hetty was artful and
how much was artless I still could not tell.

I was quite aware too, that, though Richard and Molly
were not snobs, Hetty being Lady Anybody gave her a tempo-
rary certificate, and that only goes to show. While all these
thoughts floated round my head, other thoughts came blowing
in from another direction. I knew that I was not behaving in a
spontaneous manner and certainly not exhibiting any social
grace. Would Rick think that I was a spoil-sport? Would he
feel that perhaps he had erred, dear Rick, in making it easy to
include my lovely friend, when perhaps I was not in the
humour for an association with happier days in Lytton? Or
would Rick even think that I was jealous of Lady Connot?
Because certainly Hetty by reason of being herself, and not by
anything she said, was restfully absorbing the whole party, and
I found myself engaged in eating my steak, and listening to
the laughter of Molly, and to the voice of Rick and to the rare
slow phrases of Hetty, and watching her face.

It was Hetty who, looking at her small be-jewelled watch,
said she must go. "But, Frankie," she exclaimed, "when shall I
see you again? I wish I were going with you to Paris tomor-
row! What fun we should have!" ("Yes," I thought, "I wish you
were going, too, Hetty. I'd like to have you under my eye!") "I
will give you my address, Frankie." Now the helpless fingers,
and vaguely, "Has someone a pencil?" Of course Rick had a
pencil, and he wrote Hetty's address on a card and gave it to
me; and of course he learned it off by heart, and so, you could
see, did the charmed Molly.

"And Frankie's address!" said Hetty. And Rick wrote my
address on another card, and gave it to her. There we were.

Richard hailed a taxi and we all got in. "What a lovely party," my mind echoed gloomily. Many a fond good-bye was said as I was dropped at Thos. Cook's to meet Paula. Rick and Molly would take Lady Connot wherever she wanted to go, and that seemed to suit her very well. So away went the taxi, with most of my joy and Hetty Dorval, and I went in to meet Paula in a rare state of perturbation. *How foolish, to feel so uneasy. Molly has to meet people like Hetty some time, no doubt. But not now, not now, and not through me. And as for Richard . . .*

Paula was very sweet when she found me absent-minded. She knew, of course, about Father.

TWELVE

When I got back to my boarding-house it was dinnertime and I went straight to the telephone in the hall. This was going to be difficult, very unprivate in the hall. "Rick," I was going to say, "Look, I think I should tell you that the charming person we met this afternoon isn't really a friend of mine though she sounded like it. I'm telling you this on account of Molly. She charms birds off trees, but truly I don't think you'd like . . . I mean I don't know an awful lot about her, but I'm telling you that I think she's no good . . ." and maundering on like that, not disturbing the memory of the late Sir Terence particularly. All I knew against Hetty was hearsay except for her two semi-admissions to me, once when I was a child and said good-bye to her years ago in Lytton, and again in her hurried secret words on the ship – and of course her note was also some kind of admission. I told myself, "Oh no, it was not Richard whom I was warning off Hetty, but Richard for Molly." And having had that warning, for Molly of course, Richard would have to do what he liked about it. I shut firmly away any personal concern about Richard. Perhaps.

I heard the bell ring in Rick's rooms, the little strident sound shrilling to the empty air. Rick and Molly had not returned. And when I telephoned again late at night they still had not returned. The very fact of ringing had eased my mind a bit, as if telephoning could of itself constitute a sort of warning to them. I finished packing, went to bed, fell asleep, and at about three o'clock woke up, awake at once, and filled with apprehensions. At that dread hour when the normal swells and darkens to the tentacled abnormal; when a sore throat or a pain in the chest leads logically to death, burial and disintegration; when an omission becomes a disaster; when a mishap to the beloved one becomes fatal – at that dread hour I sat up in bed and looked into the darkness and saw the amiable Hetty menacing our peace. The pattern fell into place again on the black and invisible counterpane – "*Frankie!*" with delight, "Is your Mother in England?" and softly, "You know that Terence died?", the emanating look, and the facts that an hour later Hetty was whisked away by Rick and Molly, that Molly was in an obvious state of incipient infatuation, while I, who was the only person who had reason to think that Hetty was poison, was leaving for Paris at once. It was I who had unintentionally brought them together, but it would be my responsibility if they – or Richard – were not warned. I could see Rick looking at me crossly, "Why didn't you tell me? Because Molly . . ." And yet, warn Richard? Suddenly that seemed fatuous and insulting. Was Rick to be protected from Hetty Dorval by me, an inexperienced schoolgirl with very little to offer in proof? Nevertheless, I argued with myself, if seven years ago Father was thoroughly upset because I went to see Hetty, I was certainly right in assuming that she was not a good person for Molly to become fond of. "Oh but," said that other self who sits opposite and argues disturbingly at three o'clock in the morning, "that was all a very long time ago; are you going to continue to hold an old story, of which you indeed know nothing, against Hetty forever?" I needed that sane little arbiter, my mother. And when I thought of Mother, all constancy, courage and sparkling sincerity, up came the words, "Good is as visible as green." In my mother, good was visible. I thought of others in whom good was as visible as green, but it was not visible in Hetty. I could not see Hetty plainly. I could not tell what Hetty was really like. I was subject to all her charm, but I felt no confidence in her. I would stop agitating myself, I would lie down. I would go to sleep. I would not be an idiot. I would turn over on my right. I would turn over on my left. I would telephone Rick first thing in the morning. I would not telephone Rick at all. I was making much out of nothing. Hetty was not so insidiously potent. I was all cockeyed, yet I needed advice. But Rick was off to Edinburgh at once and Molly was going home. They would never see Hetty again, and if they did, what did it matter? I would telephone Rick. Oh, go to sleep! You're off to Paris in the morning!

Before Paula's father called for me, after early breakfast, I again telephoned to Rick's room, feeling by this time rather self-conscious and a simpleton; because with London daylight, and tea and toast, and traffic in the streets, Hetty Dorval had dwindled to moderate size. However, telephoning made no difference because the small voice told me aggravatingly that the line was out of order. Thus the Telephone Company took the fates of several people straight out of my hands. However, I thought, I shall drop a line to Rick in Edinburgh, and then I can do no more and shall enjoy Paris with Paula Fairfax, with never a faint nor stirring thought of Hetty Dorval . . . "Oh, Mr. Fairfax, there you are, isn't it thrilling?

Hello, Paula, how many have you got? I have two and the
hatbox!" Oh, beaming sun and frabjus day! Along Bayswater
Terrace! Into the Bayswater Road! Into the train! Here's
Newhaven; here's the Channel and the grey waves tossing
indifferently; here's Dieppe, the Customs, the train filled with
French people, the air filled with the French language. Paris!
Paula, isn't it divine? – And I forgot to write to Rick until we'd
been in Paris for nearly a week.

"Dear Rick," I then wrote all in a rush, "I meant to tell
you before I left, but I hadn't a chance, that Lady Connot isn't
as much of a friend of mine as she sounded. But she used to
be at Lytton and . . ." And what? But I forged ahead and said
that Lady Connot was probably not a good friend for Molly.
I boggled at words like reputation and mistress and even
Shanghai, because they looked so damning when written,
much worse than if I had spoken them. But I damned her a
bit just the same and, that done, wrote about Paris. I mailed
the letter to Rick care of Gillespie & Gillespie, Engineering
Works, with their office on Princes Street, to catch him in
Edinburgh, and then forgot that Hetty existed.

And then, three weeks later, bang! – two letters arrived
by the same post that turned my three-o'clock-in-the-morning
fears to true malignant prophecy, and up rose Hetty blotting
out with her blasted good looks the Arc de Triomphe, the
bridges of the Seine and the gargoyles on Notre Dame. And
Cliff House.

Richard had not gone to Edinburgh after all, Molly told
me, and so she had stayed up in town with him for ten days.
And they had seen Lady Connot every single day and wasn't
she wonderful? And she (Hetty) had told her (Molly) to call
her "Hetty." And every evening they had been to the theatre
or dancing or had just gone to Hetty's and Hetty had sung all

evening. Wasn't that heavenly? (*Yes, indeed, Molly, I remember well, it was.*) And next holidays Rick was going to bring her down to Cliff House. "And Frankie, I do believe Rick's fallen in love at last. And isn't she brave, because her husband had only his pension?" And on and on for six heart-sinking pages.

And then a letter from Mother. Mother was still in Victoria but it was plain that she wanted to be at home again. "I shall stay here," she wrote in her usual galloping way, "till May when Jean will come to me again and we will go to the ranch and help to see Mr. Baker over the summer. He may buy the ranch next year Frankie – I don't know. I haven't quite made up my mind. How do you feel about it? But if I do sell it I shall put the little bungalow in order and get it ready for you and me to live in when you come back. At least, I shall live there darling and you shall come and go as you will. Wasn't it extraordinary, Frankie, that Father and you and I were all there together then that one day, and that Father saw it and looked at those very hills and ate his lunch there and even lay down and slept there? I'm so thankful. I can't explain but that makes the bungalow into home for me. I shan't feel a bit strange there dear. Oh Frankie the bungalow reminds me. You remember The Menace? Dear dear what an afternoon! I had tea with Eleanor and a friend of hers from Shanghai, a Mrs. Kennerly-Corbett, and she and Eleanor spoke of a school friend and Eleanor said She married a Frenchman in Shanghai didn't she, and Mrs. K-C said My Dear Didn't You Know and Eleanor said No what? And then Mrs. K-C really began. It doesn't matter telling you because Mrs. K-C would tell anyone with pleasure. And here's the story as she told it to us.

"Eleanor's friend and her husband were awfully happy, a sweet couple, and they rode a lot and kept their horses at a riding stable. And then the girl was going to have a baby and

didn't ride so much and just at that time a most beautiful creature came from goodness knows where and gave lessons at this
riding stable. And my dear this young Frenchman went completely mad about her and it appears that he left his wife and
the girl lived with him and then dreadful things happened and
in the end the wife, Eleanor's friend, took her own life, she was
so unhappy. And then of course the husband was distracted
but the girl calmly left him and went away without any
warning on one of the *Empress* boats with a rich oil man. She
was a most extraordinary girl, Mrs. K-C said, because some
people knew her and said that simply if a situation wasn't
pleasant she just walked out on it wherever she was and
nothing and nobody else disturbed her – their feelings I mean.
And Mrs. K-C said how lovely she was to look at and with an
angel face and a selfish monster and suddenly I thought, Mrs.
Dorval! And then Mrs. K-C said to me Oh don't you come
from the Upper Country? We heard that she didn't go with
this man to California at all but that he set her up somewhere
in British Columbia where the riding was good and then for
some reason she up and left him. So I said Yes that must be
Mrs. Dorval. But she said she didn't think Dorval was the
name but it must have been the same because I described her.
I told her that as far as I knew she was married now. Mrs. K-
C was frightfully excited to think that I'd actually seen her and
knew of her. Eleanor kept on saying How awful, poor Jeannie.
She really is astounding, Mrs. Dorval I mean, to have lived
through so much storm and fury and caused it too, and not a
sign on her face. She simply can't *mind*. I wonder if you'll ever
see her again."

By this time Mother must have received a letter from
me, crossing hers, telling her about meeting Hetty but not
stressing it much. Things always look more important or more

foolish, you never can tell which, when they're written, and I had not enlarged on the implications of the meeting.

Now what to do? Probably Rick had never received my letter, but if he had, *after* he'd fallen for Hetty, how he would loathe me.

Paula put her head into my room. "Well? Finished? Hurry up. Aren't you coming out?" and then she came in and stood looking at me. "Why, what's the matter?"

"Oh, Paula," I said, "I think I'll tell you all about it." And I did, from the first time that I rode with Hetty over the sage and along the dusty road from Lillooet, down to the time that she went off in the cab with Richard and Molly, right down to Molly's revealing exuberant letter, and to Mother's story.

Paula regarded me with her hard, wise, impudent face grown serious. "What shall I do?" I said. "I'll *have* to go back, Paula. I've got to see Hetty. I can't see Rick now, he'll just hate me. And I couldn't do anything with Molly. Uncle David, perhaps. No, I've got to see Hetty but probably the harm's done. If it is harm, and I think it is."

"Frankie, you must go, at once," said Paula. "We'll go out and get your tickets now and you beat it. That's what you'll do."

I left for England.

THIRTEEN

As the train slid towards London I recognized within myself from time to time the startling nature of this journey for me, inexperienced as I was. At some moments I seemed to be a straw in a stream of cause and effect; but I knew that this was not so and that the very nature and strength of the decision to leave a planned course and come to London alone, to tackle the experienced Hetty alone and try to see her as she was, and to battle her if necessary showed that I had more force than I had given myself credit for. This gave confidence. But Hetty was *terra incognita* and I could not yet estimate my powers there. I said to myself: "Hetty arms herself in silence and withdrawal. So can you. Don't let her silence reach you." The strength of Hetty's silence would be this – that her friend (could she really have a friend?) or lover or antagonist would waste himself in emotion and talk, and Hetty would remain serene and unwasted. Having taken the decision to come to London and seek her out, I no longer felt adolescent. I was armed and adequate, but I was wary enough to suspect the queer exhilaration that I felt. This exhilaration did not come from any power that new knowledge of Hetty had given me. I was not even glad to have this power because, mistrust her as I might, I yet could not dislike Hetty and did not escape from her attraction. The knowledge which I had, served only to make clear my way. The situation had resolved itself. There was Cliff House, infused always by the mutual trust and affection of people who would never expose each other to grief or shame. And there was Hetty who did not feel the responsibility that love engenders, and for whose complete selfishness her beauty and charm could not atone. Hetty could enter a life and then leave it like the seven devils. And I was sure that if Hetty in an idle or lonely moment entered the integrity of Cliff House, she would later as idly depart and leave wreckage behind. And it would be on Rick that the desolation would chiefly fall. Feeling along this frightening unfamiliar path I found a touchstone. If, when I should see Hetty and show her my mind, she should become either angry or distressed, then I should have to believe that in so far as Hetty could be moved, she was moved. I should then have to believe that she loved Richard, and – although she knew what knowledge I held – that she still was determined to marry him and perhaps to make and to keep him happy. But if Hetty should look at me with her gentle unrevealing look and keep silent, and, presently, rise and leave me and shut a door between us, then it would be plain that Hetty remained the Hetty of Shanghai and of Lytton and of how many more places, and that Menace was still her true name. That, at all events, was the way that the light shone on the path I had taken and was now treading.

Rain fell pattering on the shining pavements as I left my room to seek out Hetty that evening. Dark branches were silhouetted against the street lights and there was the satisfactory feeling of an easy rain that always brought a sense of well-being. Familiar London growled gently about me for miles. In Paris, Paula and I, being only strangers and students, had not experienced the impending feeling which we had felt in London and which I now felt again. From London we drew in the significant emanations of time past and time to come with our breath, and they entered our blood, brains and spirit. Sometimes in Piccadilly or in Whitehall I had become aghast at the pre-vision of craters, rubble and death. *For what are you destined, you arrogant man, walking unhurriedly along St. James's Street? And you, you rolling bus with your load? And you, hurrying waiter? What awaits us all?* But as I walked through the rain in Hyde Park to take my bus to Hetty's, the skies above London were still empty. Paula's father was a journalist, whose territory was Middle Europe, and from him Paula and I had caught the feeling of pre-vision with the on-coming months, but more than anywhere in London, which speaks through air and stone, wall and pavement.

I did not hurry on my way nor did I feel anxious lest Hetty should be out. If she were out, then I would stay until she came in. But to telephone to her, and to try to arrange a meeting would have been folly, for she would then, I felt, vanish between empty finger-tips. It was not easy in the dark rainy streets to find the tall house where Hetty had her small apartment; but when I had found it, was admitted, stood in my wet mackintosh at her door and rang the bell, and Mouse opened the door, I thought *This Is It*.

Unquestionably Mrs. Broom did not know me. Seven years ago she had seen me as a superfluous visiting child. Three years ago she no doubt had observed me in her own contemp-tuous way on board ship. And here I was, a young woman with some confidence who had not, it seemed, crossed her path before. On Mrs. Broom's side there was also a change.

She had grown thinner, and, under the hall light, age and perhaps fatigue showed in her face, but the iron grey of her hair was the same. The look on Mrs. Broom's face was still the contained look of a woman who, one might think, consumed herself in unhappiness. She had the look of a woman who defended, and was at all points wary, and closed herself in from all people.

"Mrs. Broom," I said, "I should like to see Hetty." Mrs. Broom looked at me as though this were a statement whose implications were to be considered. She had developed the manner of being about to close a door on you to a very high degree since I had seen her in Lytton.

"Who are you and what is your business?" she asked. Her cold eyes examined me.

"I am Frankie Burnaby, and I wish to see Hetty," I answered, not thinking it at all strange that Mrs. Dorval and Lady Connot should now be, as far as I was concerned, simply Hetty.

There was no greeting from Mrs. Broom. Indeed, if there was a change in her expression it became more defending than before. "Burnaby?" she said, and then "Oh," and we stood and looked at each other. "And your business?"

"I wish to see Hetty," I answered again without explanation. *I'm not afraid of you, you formidable woman with your pretence of power and withdrawal. Withdrawal, like Hetty's, but not beautiful. I have it in me to feel sorry for you, you cold stern woman, now that I see you again and am not afraid of you any more.*

Mrs. Broom said, "I will see," and almost, but not quite, closed the door, leaving me standing.

I did not push my way in, but all the same I walked in, and followed Mrs. Broom into the small hall. She turned angrily. "I told you I would see. You may wait outside the door," she said.

"I will wait here," I said, smiling at Mrs. Broom, who did not smile at me.

This time Mrs. Broom closed the door through which she went. I was glad, I was quite happy that here, near me, was Hetty, and with Hetty a clearing up of things, or this new Me that waited in the hall was strangely deluded. So little doubt had I that I should see her soon, now, that I had taken off my wet mackintosh and laid it over a chair in the small hall. There was no sign of any other visitor. If Hetty was there, she was probably alone. Good.

Mrs. Broom returned, closing the door. ("Does this woman do nothing but close doors all her life?" I thought – and indeed the closing of doors typified Mrs. Broom.) "Lady Connot is not able to see you this evening. She has an engagement. You will have to come again," she said. Not I. But the door that Mrs. Broom had shut, now opened, and Hetty stood there. "Mouse, don't be ridiculous," she said. (I had heard those words before but this time Hetty's light voice did not reduce me to a faltering schoolgirl.) "Frankie! Come in. What luck! I have just a few minutes and then I'm being called for. I thought you were still in Paris! How nice of you to come! Sit down," and she indicated a chair. I do not know whether Mrs. Broom left the room or whether she stood back in the shadow. I think she stood in the shadow, but I forgot her.

"Yes, I was in Paris," I said.

I looked round the room. We both stood, Hetty in front of a low couch, and I beside a chair. A fire burned in the narrow English grate. On a table stood a lamp which threw light upwards on to the ceiling and downwards on to the table. As Hetty stood, her face was in the dark interval of space between light and light, and I suppose mine was too. And so we stood looking at each other. Hetty laughed. "Well, Frankie, aren't you going to sit down? I shall. For a few minutes." And she sat on the couch, and the soft firelight and lamplight showed me her face, as young and unworn as when I first saw her seven years before on the Lillooet road.

"*What* is it, Frankie?" she asked beguilingly, "you funny child. You appear – I remember before – with the air of one making portentous announcements. Is it your rôle? You have become too serious, Frankie. Wasn't Paris gay enough? I like your hair. It looks very nice. Very smart. Pull up that fat little chair."

This sweet clever Hetty had put the room at ease at once, but I was not to be deflected.

"Yes," I said, "Paris was all right. But as your time is short, Hetty, I'll come to the point at once." I was still standing. "Yesterday, in Paris, two letters came, and they were both about you. One was from my little Molly, Molly Trethewey, and one was from Canada. Molly's letter told me all about the last few weeks and I can see that you and Rick and Molly – and particularly you and Richard – have become great . . . friends." I was watching Hetty closely. "The letter from Canada told me about your last year in Shanghai, and about your coming to Canada." Her expression did not change. "Now, I don't mind what you've done, or where you've been, or who you've lived with or how you've left them, until it touches Richard – and Molly. And I've come to ask you. Have you decided to marry Richard Trethewey?"

Hetty looked up at me with gentle bright amusement. "Oh, Frankie, you *are* funny, you know! Darling, you're so droll and serious! Have you come all the way from Paris to ask me my intentions? You've been reading too many stories.

Please. *Please!* Don't be sentimental, Frankie, or heroic. I shall only think you're funny!" Hetty was pricking my little balloons, and smiling as she pricked.

"I shan't be sentimental or heroic, Hetty," I said, feeling quite good-humoured. This didn't get under my skin at all. "I simply need to be told whether you intend to marry Richard. And this is why, if you'd like to know. Because, *now*, I truly believe you're as selfish as a human being can be, and my friends at Cliff House are too good to be made unhappy by you. So there!" I said defiantly.

Hetty leaned forward, her hands clasped over her knees. She seemed to be quite interested and not at all annoyed.

"You think you simply need to know whether I intend to marry Richard?" She laughed. "My dear child, my dear little prig, you don't simply need that at all. You're in love with Richard yourself and you're very jealous." Under the brilliance of Hetty's amused gaze perhaps I coloured.

"I don't know, Hetty." I thought for a minute. "Perhaps I am in love with Rick. I think I am. But I can tell you this. I'm not jealous of you and I never could be. You can believe that – though, in fact, I don't care whether you do or not. If you marry Rick without being in love with him, if you marry him because you're . . . bored or . . . lonely or for 'security' again (aren't you secure now?) you'll let him down and you'll break Rick's heart. You will!" I moved over and leaned towards her, with my hands on the table beyond the wide circle of lamplight. "Do you *intend* to marry him? *Do* you?"

Hetty looked at me with her soft, untroubled, unrevealing look but did not answer.

I drew a long breath. "Well, then," I said, "suppose you intend to marry Rick. Molly will be in your charge." I pondered this, looking at Hetty, who gave no sign. I had never taken my eyes off her, and I tried to read her face. I could not read it.

"Hetty, it all rests on this, and you must tell me . . . do you love him, and will you stick to him if you marry him?"

Hetty did not answer. Her face was as calm and sweetly inexpressive as though she sat alone and a vehement young woman were not standing near her. Vehement, I say. Yet it was a fact that there was not the making of a quarrel at that time in the room, and that neither Hetty nor I appeared angry. We both waited in silence for the other and my own words sounded strangely in my ears. I assumed that Richard was in love with Hetty although she had not told me this, and, of course, neither had he. But it was an easy assumption.

Hetty disregarded my question and did not answer it.

"Frankie," she said slowly, "you wrote to Richard, didn't you?"

I nodded. "Yes," I said, "I took particular pains to tell Richard soon after we met you that I never knew you well, and that's true too, and I – well, I put him on his guard about you, Hetty. That's the truth."

"I know," she said, without rancour. "Rick only got the letter this week. He was angry, Frankie, because he had got to know me well by then, you see," she said gently. Yes. I saw.

Hetty then showed what she thought was pity. "That letter won't help you with Rick, you know, Frankie. He'll never like you now. Not ever."

I said rather hotly, "If you think that letter was written in order to help *me* with Richard, then you still don't know what this conversation is about." I pulled myself together. I could not afford to get angry.

"Since we're talking – and *don't* you hate scenes, don't let's have a scene, Frankie, –" she said in her beguiling way. "If

I decide to marry Rick, what do you intend to do with your Shanghai stories?" and she also watched me intently.

I waited a minute, and then I had to hand Hetty an advantage.

"Do you think I shall tell tales on Rick's wife?" I said. "You can answer that one yourself." That was the only truthful answer I could find to Hetty's question.

There was one more thing to be said in this so far inconclusive talk.

"Hetty," I said, "*if* you marry Rick, and I don't think you actually will, because you're a realist where your own comfort's concerned," (I had discussed that part with Paula) "and you know that you'd hate to take on responsibilities in a married life with a man like Rick with a little sister like Molly . . . because Molly's part of Rick's life . . . you'd have to keep it up, and you'd get bored, and you'd hate that – but if you *do* marry him, what will you do about Molly? She'll be your care, too. You'll be her sister, but you'll have to be more like her mother. I know all this so well, Hetty, because I've lived with them so much – and Molly's never had a mother."

And here Hetty made the mistake of her life. She laughed and said lightly, "*I* never had a mother, either, and I've got on very nicely without one!"

It was at that moment that Mrs. Broom moved forward out of the shadows and stood and leaned with her strong rough hands on the table in the circle of the lamplight. The whole room seemed to turn towards her, and we turned towards her, and she took all the power and meaning out of the room into herself. And she began to shake.

Hetty and I stared at this controlled woman who stood shaking by the table, steadying herself with her strong hands flat on the table within the circle of the lamplight. I stood up

straight and saw her hands square and rough and the fingers
short and square-tipped pressed down hard upon the table to
prevent their shaking as Mrs. Broom was shaking. The lower
part of Mrs. Broom's face was in shadow but on her forehead
I saw the veins stand out on the temples and then I saw that
the whole face was distorted. I cannot tell you how horrible
this was and how frightening, to see this woman of wood and
of closed doors opened violently from within with great sud-
denness and without reason. Hetty put her hands on the
couch on each side of her and leaned backwards as though to
spring away. She looked in horror at Mrs. Broom who, still
leaning forward on the table, struggled to compose herself.

"Mouse, what is it?" breathed Hetty. "What is it?"

I did not put out a hand to help Mrs. Broom because I
saw that though she was racked and shaken physically, the
thing that had caused this convulsion was not physical – and
I did not know what it was.

Mrs. Broom spoke to Hetty, hoarsely and with effort.
"Say what you said before!"

"What I said before?" said Hetty, bewildered. "I don't
know what I said before."

"Then I'll tell you," said Mrs. Broom, who was gaining
control of herself. "You said, 'I never had a mother, and I got
along very well without one.'"

"Well, I *did* get along very well without one – thanks to
you of course, Mouse," added Hetty generously.

Mrs. Broom looked on Hetty and said, "Hester . . . I am
your mother," and the silence in the room was as though
drums had stopped beating.

Hetty went quite white and stared at Mrs. Broom as
though she had never seen her before, and perhaps she never
had. I saw her breast heave as though she had been running.

"Mouse," she said at last, "that's not true!"

"Hester, I am your mother," repeated Mrs. Broom sombrely. "Many's the time I've near told you and now I've done it."

"Why . . ." said Hetty, and then she stopped. "Who . . ." And she stopped again. "Mouse, you can't prove it!"

"Prove it!" said Mrs. Broom scornfully, "I've no call to prove it. I don't have to prove it. You're my daughter, Hester, and you've brought me nothing but trouble from the minute you could speak and you've never given me any real love."

Hetty's mind was set on something. She didn't seem to listen. She looked through the room, through the walls, and concentrated on something.

"Then who is my father?" she said at last, looking up at Mrs. Broom, and I found myself sorry for Hetty. If there was a side, I was on Hetty's side.

"*You'd like to know!*" said Mrs. Broom with gathered anger and scorn, and the words un-dammed and began to flow. "You'd like to know who your father is and you'll never know! I'll never tell you! He done all right by you and it was his money you lived by till you was twenty-one and after, and it was his money edjcated you well, and if I loosed you on him now, he and his would never know another happy minute from you . . . he's pretty near forgotten about me and about you too by now. And you've led me to trouble and hard work and shame of you, and me always your servant. I pretty near left you in Hongkong, and pretty near left you in Shanghai, and Lytton, and Vancouver, and Montreal. You near drove me to it but I stayed by you and by you and now you'd marry this man and bring the same to these decent people as you done to me. I'll tell him first that you're rotten bad and selfish and see how he likes it. *You done all right without a mother.*" The bitterness that Mrs. Broom put into those words was ferocious.

Hetty had shrunk back on the couch as though she had been struck and I was sorry for her. Like a fool I was so sorry for her that I spoke to Mrs. Broom. Like a fool indeed.

"Oh, Mrs. Broom," I said, "why did you do this to Hetty now? Why did you let Hetty grow up like this, all in the dark . . . ? If you'd brought her up like mother and daughter maybe she'd . . ."

She flashed round at me. "A lot you know, you comfortable safe ones. Wait till you've had your baby in secret, my fine girl, in a dirty foreign place, and found a way to keep her sweet and clean and a lady like her father's people was, before you talk so loud. Shut your mouth!"

Hetty put her hands to her head. She smoothed her hands over her eyes and forehead, over and over, mechanically. And then a bell rang in the house. Again . . . again . . . the bell rang again. I do not think that Mrs. Broom or Hetty even heard this loud jangling bell, and I did not stir. Mrs. Broom looked with great intensity at Hetty, whose eyes were closed. "Oh, do what you like," she said in an anguish, "marry who you like and where you want to. I've done. I'm tired. I'm going. I'm not going to follow your damned dance any more. You're not sorry for *me*, Hester. You're not giving me a thought. You never have and you never will, not to nobody." And she stood there, still leaning upon the table, looking at Hetty with grief and need.

And Hetty did exactly what Hetty would do. She did not speak to her mother. Without a word or a look she rose and slowly went out of the room, closing the door behind her, and left her mother standing there, looking after her with a ravaged face.

Mrs. Broom had forgotten me. She now looked down at her hands, and so did I. Her hands, with the pressure upon the table, were red and looked swollen and congested. She held up her hands and regarded them strangely, turning their roughness this way and that to the light. What she thought as she regarded her worn hands so strangely I could only guess.

As Mrs. Broom seemed oblivious of me, and I am sure that she was, I found myself no longer necessary to this situation. I went into the hall and put on my mackintosh, very much astonished. She, lost in her own dreadful moment, neither saw nor heard me go.

While Mrs. Broom and I had stood there in silence, I had heard a telephone bell ring in what seemed to be Hetty's room. Perhaps she had answered it. I did not know. I heard no voice. When I opened the front door to go out again into the rain, I almost ran into Rick, who saw me in the light of the street lamp and stopped suddenly. I closed the door behind me and the lock clicked.

"What are *you* doing here?" Rick said to me angrily.

"Oh hello, Rick," I said, "Was that you ringing? I heard someone ringing."

"Yes, and no one came. I saw the lights on up there and I knew there was someone in and I went and telephoned and Hetty told me not to come . . . So I came. What are you doing here, Frankie? Why aren't you in Paris? Why did you write me that letter? By the way, I tore it up. Please don't meddle in my business."

"Rick," I said, "when I wrote you that letter Hetty wasn't your business. She was my business. Let me go. It's raining. I'm going home."

Rick stood square in front of me. "You've got to tell me what brought you here tonight. When I saw Hetty yesterday we arranged definitely that I should call for her tonight. There was no word of you coming then. And now you're here – and when I telephoned now she told me to go away and then she hung up. Frankie, you're a devil! Why *are* you here? You're up to something." Rick was very angry and I must say it was a queer spot to be in. I had never seen him like this before. But I'd seen something tonight that made me not care.

I stuck my hands in my mackintosh pockets and there we stood in the rain, Rick blocking my way and glowering. "Well," I said, "Rick, I had business with Hetty that arose – yesterday. And it had to be settled at once."

"What business?"

"My business was with Hetty," I said as coldly as I knew how, "and you can just stop hectoring me like this. But I'll tell you something. Mrs. Broom and Hetty have had a row and I think Mrs. Broom will leave Hetty – or Hetty will leave Mrs. Broom more likely."

"Mrs. Broom leave her?" said Richard, "she never will. She's devoted to her! Hetty! Poor kid!" And he made a move as if to ring the bell again.

I put my hand on his arm. "Rick," I said very earnestly, "there's trouble between Hetty and Mrs. Broom and if you try to go in – well, they just won't let you in. They're not thinking about you now. I'm telling you, Rick. Now I'm going – no, I'll take myself home, thank you, I don't feel like having your company," – not that he had shown any sign of taking me home, but I was going to get that in first – and I started down the steps, thinking that this was a good note on which to leave him. I looked back, though, and when I saw Rick standing there, I stopped and said, "Rick! Don't start thinking that Hetty's unhappy and that her heart is broken and that you have to do something about it. Believe me, Hetty's heart has never broken yet, and it's not going to begin now. Goodnight, dear Rick."

I don't know whether he heard what I said or cared what I said, because he turned away impatiently and applied himself again to the business of getting into the house. And I went home.

I walked all the way and got to my room wet through and pretty tired. I was devastated too, because take it whichever way you like, Rick was going to be very unhappy – and so was I, as far as I could see.

FOURTEEN

When I got back to my room at Mrs. Plant's I unpacked my bag and got ready for bed but I did not go to bed at once. I sat in the one comfortable chair smoking cigarette after cigarette. Lying back watching the sinuous, sensuous, slow convolutions of smoke rising and establishing a soft impalpable grey ceiling above me, in which I all but lost my thoughts, I contemplated the strange and poignant situation of Mrs. Broom. The focus of the *affaire Hetty* had shifted. I could not imagine what new relation would exist between mother and daughter. I wanted Paula to talk to, it was all so extraordinary. Or Mother. Although I had not thought of Mother and Father in relation to this whole matter, I am sure now that it was they who had been the unconscious or subconscious cause of my intervention, which in itself was a fight on behalf of Rick, whether he liked it or not. In this thankless and questionable fight I had handled dynamite, and in so doing had exploded the hidden mine of Mrs. Broom to my own great astonishment ("No man is an Iland,").

I had just stood up ready to go to bed, when there was a knock at the door and the not very pleased face of Mrs. Plant looked in. "There's a lady coming to see you, Miss Burnaby," she said in her own particular tone of asperity, and naturally, for it was too late for visitors. She had gone to bed and had had to get up. And then came Hetty into the room, wonderfully smart and careless. Mrs. Plant gave her a look, and left.

"Hetty!" I said amazed, and perhaps my expression resembled Mrs. Plant's because Hetty said, "Yes, I know, Frankie. But you've no *idea* how dreadful it's been. Mouse was *frightful* to me." And Hetty's eyes were starry and her eyebrows piteous, but her voice was still light and indolent; nothing headlong, nothing lost, nothing distraught about this one who had left a woman in ruins. Hetty sank into the chair and dropped furs, bag, gloves. Gloves, I thought! How curious and how like her that Hetty remembered to bring her gloves. She took off her little hat and dropped that too and smoothed back the fair hair.

"Did you see Rick?" I asked quickly.

"Rick?" said Hetty vaguely. "Oh no, that was *too* much, what was the good? I didn't want . . . and I knew, Frankie, you'd give me a bed. I almost thought . . . Oh," as her eyes strayed around the room and she saw its plainness, "just that bed? . . . But it'll do for tonight," she said naïvely. "I knew you wouldn't mind, Frankie."

And so it was that very soon Hetty was sitting up in my bed, dressed in my best night-dress and saying, "You know, Frankie, I liked your mother." *Did you? You never knew my mother.* But Hetty took the words out of my mind, "I never knew her, of course, but I observed her on the boat. Your mother's good, Frankie, and she's funny too. Amusing, I mean. She'd be fun to be with. I really wish I'd known her in Lytton."

"Mother's a darling, she –" I began, and stopped. I couldn't talk to Hetty, of all people, about my mother – then.

Hetty looked beyond me. "Do you remember that mare I had in Lytton? Juniper? Wasn't she a beauty? Sometimes when the moon was full I used to saddle Juniper and ride at night down to the Bridge, and across, and up the Lillooet road and off into the hills. And Frankie, it was so queer and beautiful and like nothing else. Though there was nothing round you but the hills and the sage, all very still except for the sound of the river, you felt life in everything and in the moon too. All the shapes different at night. And such stars. And once in the moonlight the geese going over. I remember the shadows the moonlight made on the ground, great round sage-bushes all changed at night into something alive, and everything else silver. And once or twice the northern lights – yes, really. And then the coyotes baying in the hills to the moon – all together, do you remember, Frankie, such queer high yelling as they made, on, and on, and on?"

Yes, I remembered, standing there in London at the foot of a small shabby brass bedstead listening to Hetty, looking at her and wondering, "Do nocturnal animals feel like that? What is Hetty?" I remembered the yelling of the coyotes in the hills, and the moon shining on the hills and on the river; the smell of the sage; and the sudden silence as the coyotes stopped for a moment in their singing all together. I remembered the two coloured rivers. And my home. What a strange Hetty, after such an evening, calling up this magic – for it was a disturbing magic to me, the genius of my home – and Hetty's smart wrinkly gloves lying on the floor, her little black hat lying there too. I remembered Lytton, and the rivers, and the Bridge, all as real as ever in British Columbia while we looked at each other in London, yet saw them plainly.

As she talked, the hard light of the badly shaded electric bulb above my bed shone upon Hetty's face and then I saw the lines, faintly. But they were there. Her clever make-up was not there, and she no longer looked ageless, but a little old. "Mouse didn't like me to take those rides, she was afraid of Indians or animals or something. And Juniper was often nervous. But I never loved anything so much in all my life, Frankie. It sounds ridiculous, but I never felt so *free*, before or since. You know . . . *people* . . ." and her voice trailed off.

The word "Mouse," spoken casually and with no emotion at all, reminded me and made me angry. Hetty was here, inescapable, for the night. After that I had done with her. Finished. "Move over, Hetty," I said crossly, "I've got to get to sleep," and I got in.

"Yes, Frankie," said Hetty as docile as a child. She turned over in bed and made a beautiful S with herself that nearly pushed me out, and settled herself to sleep. I looked down at her in mystification, for almost before I had time to turn out the light, this woman, whose mind should have been full of consuming sorrow or of rage or even of compassion, was sweetly asleep, the curves of her cheek and of her lips very innocent and tender.

There is that in sleep which reduces us all to one common denominator of helplessness and vulnerable humanity. The soft rise and fall of the unconscious sleeper's breast is a miracle. It is a binding symbol of our humanity. The child in the lost attitude of sleep is all children, everywhere, in all time. A sleeping human being is all people, sleeping, everywhere since time began. There is that in the sleeper that arrests one, pitying, and that makes us all the same. The rise and the fall of the frail envelope of skin that contains the microcosm of wonder, is the touching sign. If one had an enemy, and if one saw that enemy sleeping, one might be dangerously moved in pity of spirit by what lies there, unconscious. I looked at Hetty and could almost forgive her because she was Hetty, sleeping; but that did not prevent me from prodding her and saying, "Hetty, *move* over, I've got to get to sleep!" There was a murmur, "Oh, *poor* Frankie," and she moved luxuriously nearer to her edge of the bed and I lay down and turned off the light.

Here I was, lying beside Hetty Dorval. It was really funny. *Mother, little dragon, what do you think of this?*

I lay there trying to be as comfortable as I could in one-third of my own single bed, and trying to go to sleep. Little by little Hetty relaxed into a spacious S again. I got out of bed, furious, turned back the bedclothes, woke her and said, "HETTY, MOVE OVER," and gave her an almighty smack on her round silken bottom. Hetty was very much surprised and a little plaintive, but very soon we were as we had been before. If I was to get any sleep, either she or I had to get out of that bed and sleep in the chair. I become more injured and enraged. Hetty's pleasant seduction of Richard, her base treatment of her mother, the trouble (and expense, for I had a very small allowance) to which she had put me, all became swallowed up in the magnitude of the fact that Hetty was sleeping in my bed and I was lying on the edge of it, angry and uncomfortable. And I wanted to get to sleep. Hetty asleep was Hetty peaceful so the only thing was to get out and let her have the bed. I got up, curled myself in the chair, covered myself with coats unpleasantly – the coats seemed to be all arms and legs and gaps – and at last went to sleep, rather chilly and in extreme discomfort.

I awoke slowly in a grey morning to hear soft singing. I opened my eyes and saw Hetty at my wash-basin.

"Je vais revoir ma Normandie,
Ma Normandie, my Normandie,
Je vais revoir my Normandie,
C'est le pays qui m'a donné . . ."

She did not sing loudly but very sweetly, and I never
hated singing worse. As I opened my eyes I realized that I was
stiff, but I was not going to let Hetty be sorry for me.

"Hello," I said, "you were so greedy that I slept in the
chair. I've had a marvellous night, and I feel fine. How soon
are you going?"

"I found your face cream, Frankie, do you mind?" said
Hetty, rubbing her chin with slow experienced finger-tips.
"Frankie, you *have* been sweet!" (*Oh no, I hadn't.*) "Will you
do something for me?" Her gentle effrontery was very effec-
tive. "Do run down to the telephone wherever it is and ring
up Jules Stern – he's at Claridge's – and tell him to call for me
here. At once. Before he goes. Hurry, Frankie, if you don't
mind, darling. I'll tell you after."

My impulse was to say, "Telephone your Jules Stern
yourself," but I was so anxious to get rid of Hetty, to get her
out of my sight and never see her again that I ran downstairs
in my dressing-gown, hoping that I would not meet Mrs.
Plant, who did not like dressing-gowns.

I got Claridge's, and I got through to Mr. Stern's room.
A man's voice answered, "Yes? Here Jules Stern."

"Mr. Stern," I said – here was a new world of Hetty's –
"I am speaking for Lady Connot."

"For Lady Connot? Yes? Who is speaking? That is not Mrs.
Broom?" said the voice eagerly and with foreign consonants.

But I was going to remain anonymous. "I am speaking

for Lady Connot. She would like you to call for her as soon as possible, this morning, now, she said, at this address."

"One moment, *bitte*," said Jules Stern, in a great hurry. "Yes?"

I gave him the address and then he said anxiously, "She is well? Lady Connot is not ill?"

"No," I said and I think I laughed, "Lady Connot is very well indeed."

"Ah," came a thankful breathing, "tell her I will come soon. At once." Jules Stern sounded so grateful that it was prophetic. I hung up and went back upstairs to my room. Hetty was nearly dressed. She sat down. "Well? You got him?" she asked cheerfully.

"Yes, I got him and he's coming at once, and he can't come too soon for me. I don't want you here again! You muddle up my life too much. Please, Hetty, look after your own affairs but keep away from me. I've got my own life to live and I don't want ever to see you again – *ever*," I said, feeling injured, stiff and, this morning, as hard as nails to Hetty Dorval.

"I understand *exactly*. I feel for you," said Hetty regarding me sympathetically. "It is preposterous the way other people clutter up and complicate one's life. It is my own phobia, Frankie, and I understand you . . . so well. But I must tell you about Jules. You wouldn't like him, Frankie – oh no, you'd not like Jules at all. Poor Jules was very upset, about Richard, I mean. He's never seen Rick, but of course he knew there was suddenly someone. Rick is a thousand times nicer, but it wouldn't do." Reflectively, "I see quite plainly that it wouldn't do. And young girls are all very well but . . . one can't give up one's *life*, exactly, can one? . . . And Jules has put off and put off going back to Vienna, so I think I'll go with him,

Frankie. Now. I've always longed to live in Vienna, it sounds just what I'd like – riding in the Prater – and the music, too. Jules would look awfully funny on a horse, but he doesn't need to ride. I shall ride. But he adores music. He plays magnificently. And he's terribly rich. There's something very *sweet* about Jules," she said, pulling her gloves.

"Oh, Hetty, you make me sick!" I said angrily, and then I stopped, glad that Rick was free of this woman, trouble or no, since she preferred the rich Jules Stern to him.

Hetty seemed very much surprised at this outburst and her eyebrows lifted in tragic gaiety. "Frankie, you're incomprehensible! I thought you'd be so pleased!" Standing there hatted and furred and gloved, she looked vaguely at the disordered room. "Darling, could I help you with the bed?" This offer was, I think, Hetty's great atonement for everything, although of course she had no intention of helping with the bed.

I pushed her out of the room. "No, no, don't help me with anything! There's a lovely horsehair sitting-room down on the first floor and you can wait there. I'm busy, busy, busy, Hetty – and I'm going back to Paris! Good-bye, good-bye." "– And oh, Hetty," I said, "don't come back for anything. If you've left something I'll throw it down to you out of the window!"

Hetty stood for one moment in the little shadowed hall facing me with a teasing pretty look. She was a picture of elegant sweetness as she stood there. Although I had fought her and driven her off, and would fight her again if I had to and defeat her, too, she was hard to hate as I looked at her. She made a gesture of good-bye and went down the stairs. (*Mrs. Broom, to what a bleak morning you awoke all alone.*)

As I watched with satisfaction Hetty going down the narrow stairs, I knew that before she had taken three steps she had forgotten me, and she had forgotten Richard. She was on her way.

Six weeks later the German Army occupied Vienna. There arose a wall of silence around the city, through which only faint confused sounds were sometimes heard.

AFTERWORD

BY NORTHROP FRYE

Ethel Wilson's work is mainly in the form of what Henry James called "the beautiful and blest novella," the short novel with a streamlined narrative aimed from the beginning at a specific resolution. *The Innocent Traveller* is longer and less shapely, doubtless because its scatterbrained gabbling heroine lasts for a hundred years. This book, however, began as Ethel Wilson's first sustained effort, and gave her an unusual amount of trouble. But *Hetty Dorval*, the two stories in *The Equations of Love, Swamp Angel*, and *Love and Salt Water* are exquisite examples of the novella form. The dénouement of *Hetty Dorval*, with its old-style recognition scene, may seem over-designed for contemporary readers accustomed to finding such things only in detective stories and the like, but perhaps contemporary tastes could do with some expanding.

Besides, it is easy to miss the real irony of Hetty Dorval's servant turning out to be her mother. Part of the irony is that Hetty is no freak in this respect: Mrs. Broom is typical of the millions of mothers of adolescent and arrested-adolescent sons or daughters who have never been recognized as anything but servants. Then again, most of us, up to a point, take

Longfellow's advice and act in the living present, but for normal people the present is at the end of the past: it is seen in a continuous temporal dimension. Hetty lives in an abstract present and her past keeps disappearing from her awareness: she can remember having seen people before but she cannot remember friendships, much less obligations. She has the charm of the self-absorbed narcissist who inspires admiration but is never touched by it, a fascination endearing in a baby or a housecat but frightening in an adult human. She is constantly spoken of as though her worst quality is her instinct to walk out of situations as soon as they involve her in responsibilities; but what makes her sinister is rather the way she walks into them. Wherever she is, some male in her orbit will move toward her, and the praying mantis will soon have another meal. But when nemesis is finally outraged beyond endurance, and confronts her with her entire past in accusation and righteous wrath, there is no melodrama: she merely stares at it innocently and waits for it to go away. It does: that is not how the Hettys of this world are caught. If they are caught, it is by totally unrelated accidents, like the one indicated unobtrusively in the last two sentences.

If the book were, as its title threatens, the story of Hetty Dorval, it might become tedious. But it is really the story of how the narrator Frankie grows from a child of thirteen into a mature woman. She has a decent father, a shrewd careful mother, and some good friends ready to help her over the rough spots. But they are dead or absent when the crisis comes, and it is Hetty, who never did anything in her life except help herself, Hetty who is not a friend but keeps turning up like an apparition in a Victorian ghost story, who actually becomes the midwife in Frankie's second birth. Of course her help is purely negative, but it is help none the less.

We first see Frankie and Hetty in the tightly constricted society of a small town in the British Columbia hinterland, where the impetuous Thompson River plunges into the devious and dangerous Fraser. Why Hetty went there and how her reputation preceded her we are not clearly told, but the fact that she is cut off from her community is mainly her own doing. No man is an island, says John Donne in the great meditation that forms the motto of the book, but Hetty is determined to be and remain an island. Frankie is naturally enchanted by a much older stranger from the outside world, and one who gives her some sense, however shallow, of what it would be like to be a complete individual in her own right. Even the pact to keep their friendship secret, though silly and creating a rift with her family, helps in a way to develop this sense. Gradually the relation changes, until at the end Hetty, temporarily in trouble, comes to Frankie and asks to share her bed, lying down in it in a (what else?) S-curve that takes up all the room. Frankie gives her a hard smack on the posterior and tells her to move over: this does not get her a fair share of the bed, naturally, but it marks the final reversal of the adult-child relation between the two.

In the background is the close proximity of nature, the *genius loci* as the author calls it, and the loving descriptions of it give the story a most distinctive beauty. But for all the beauty there is a predatory side to nature, a total indifference of every living thing to the welfare or comfort of others, with which Hetty's self-absorption blends. It is the seasonal flight of wild geese that makes the most lasting impression on both: doubtless it suggests directed flight to Frankie and simple escape to Hetty.

Hetty Dorval establishes Ethel Wilson's world, a world bounded on the west by Vancouver Island and on the east by the Okanagan valley, which links up readily with the rest of Canada and with England, but seldom crosses the United States boundary. In *Hetty Dorval* many themes are embryonic that are more deeply explored in later works. It is interesting to contrast Hetty with the heroine of "Lilly's Story" in *The Equations of Love*, who starts out as a kicked-around alleycat but forms an iron resolution to live "like folks," to achieve bourgeois respectability for herself and her daughter, and finally succeeds. She too obliterates her past, but with a vision of a future society to counterbalance it. The evocations of the British Columbia landscape, with its hills and alfalfa fields and fishing streams, have a symbolic relevance to the action, but no real "objective correlative" emerges, like the series of images which (as a somewhat defensive prefatory note tells us) are correlated with Topaz in *The Innocent Traveller*, much less anything like the revolver that gives its name to *Swamp Angel*. Carefully limited, quiet and unpretentious, *Hetty Dorval* is a typical first novel of a writer of great ability and a sure sense of direction.

BY ETHEL WILSON

FICTION

Hetty Dorval (1947)

The Innocent Traveller (1949)

The Equations of Love (1952)

Swamp Angel (1954)

Love and Salt Water (1956)

Mrs. Golightly and Other Stories (1961)

SELECTED WRITINGS

Ethel Wilson: Stories, Essays, and
Letters [ed. David Stouck] (1987)